Aubrey
and the
TERRIBLE YOOT

HORATIO CLARE

ILLUSTRATED BY
JANE MATTHEWS

Firefly

First published in 2015 by Firefly Press
25 Gabalfa Road, Llandaff North,
Cardiff, CF14 2JJ
www.fireflypress.co.uk

A CIP catalogue record of this book
is available from the British Library.

Print ISBN 9781910080283
epub ISBN 9781910080290

This book has been published with the support
of the Welsh Books Council.

Design by: Claire Brisley
Printed and bound by: Bell and Bain, Glasgow

To Robin T-S
The best lad imaginable,
from his sort-of-step-dad -
Slothinteee! Golden Hedgehog? -
This book is dedicated
With love. Xx

Horatio Clare

To Martha

Jane Matthews

CHAPTER 1

Rambunctious Boy

Aubrey's first scream was so loud it blew the wax out of his nurse's ears. All babies cry when they are born, but Aubrey's WAAAWWLL! was so fierce it also set off a doctor's car alarm.

She was an elderly nurse with a face like a kindly gargoyle. She washed him and wrapped him in a blanket.

'This child has the howl of a wolf!' the nurse exclaimed.

Aubrey took another breath and yowled so loudly he went purple. He kicked like mad too, catching the nurse a good hoof in the guts as she handed him to his mother.

'Guh!' she gasped. 'And he's...' she searched for the right word, unable to breathe until she found it, '...Rambunctious!'

The nurse could not remember the last

time she had said 'rambunctious' but she knew that it was an American word which means exactly what it sounds like. Blowing out ear wax, winding his midwife and setting off a car alarm were Aubrey's first rambunctious acts, and he achieved them in under a minute.

There is a theory that very small children subconsciously remember everything they hear. I don't know if it's true, but *Rambunctious! Wolf!* It might explain what happened next.

Next, when he was less than a year old,
Aubrey saw someone running past the
house where he lived with his parents. He
decided it was time he ran, too. At his age
wolf cubs can run marathons. Aubrey had
barely learned how to stand.

Quick! he thought, get moving!

He jumped up, threw himself forward and
flung out a leg, just like the runner. His
body kept going forward but the leg gave up
suddenly. The floor flipped up and bashed
him. He tried again, many times...

Bonk, bump, thump

...it was like listening to apples rolling off
a table.

'That's Aubrey again, smashing the
place up,' remarked Mr Ferraby with a
grin, as the thuds and blows of Aubrey's
running practice reverberated through
Woodside Terrace. The Ferrabys lived next
door. Mr Ferraby was an expert on the
astonishing array of sounds Aubrey created

as he became bigger, stronger and more adventurous.

Aubrey's parents begged him to be patient.

'Please try walking first!' implored his mother, Suzanne. Suzanne was a nurse. She knew her son was tough but she was worried he would hurt himself.

'It's the traditional next step!' his father said. Jim was an English teacher who loved stories. He was secretly delighted that his son did not seem interested in following the normal story pattern of stand, then walk, then run.

The little boy ignored them both. He specialised in ignoring Jim and Suzanne. He loved them, but you can't spend too much time listening to your parents, not if you want to live to the limit.

'Live To The Limit' was Aubrey's philosophy at this point. Having a philosophy is a very good thing, especially if it leads you on a life-saving quest.

However, having a philosophy is not such a good thing if it leads you to crash two cars before you are old enough to drive one, which was Aubrey's next trick.

When he was four years old Aubrey thought it might be fun to take the car for a spin. He had often watched his parents driving: it was easy. One Sunday afternoon, when his father was upstairs sleeping

FOOTNOTE: Aubrey's philosophy at this point is somewhere near Hedonism: live life for pleasure and excitement, nothing is more important. An ancient Greek genius called Democritus came up with the idea that contentment and happiness are the aim of a well-lived life, and if you feel them, it proves you are living well. You might feel it does not take a genius to come up with that but Democritus also came up with the idea of atoms, two thousand years before their existence was proved.

FOOTNOTE TO FOOTNOTE: Like Hedonism, atoms turn out to be something of a mixed blessing.

under one of his favourite books, and his mother was in the garden, poking around in the vegetable patch and talking to the woodpigeons, Aubrey climbed a chair and took the car key off the table. He was banned from using the front door by himself because the lane was just there, but now he did – using the chair again to reach the catch – and stepped out. He pointed the key at the car and pressed the button. The car clicked and flashed its lights at him in a friendly way.

'Hello car!' Aubrey whispered.

The view from the driving seat was mostly sky, with a steering wheel across it. He stood up on the seat: much better! He could see down the lane towards town, and he could see Rushing Wood rising up on both sides of the valley, and he could see Mr and Mrs Ferraby's smart blue German car, parked smack in front of him. He would have to go around that.

Although Aubrey forgot to put the key in

the ignition, which meant that the engine did not switch on, which meant he was never going to get very far, he did not forget to let the handbrake off. He had watched Jim and Suzanne haul it up, push the button and let it down. Aubrey did this with both hands while standing on the seat. It worked a treat. The lane just there tilts slightly down towards the town, so as soon he released the brake the car began to move.

'Yup!' cried Aubrey. It was one of his favourite words.

'YUP!' he shouted, as the car began to roll properly, and he turned the steering wheel hard to the right, because Mr and Mrs Ferraby's car was very close now and he had to go round it or –

CRUNCH!

Mr Ferraby's car began to shout and wail like a goose and a donkey having a fight - HONK HONK! - HEE HAAW! - and flash all its lights in distress.

Because Woodside Terrace is a very quiet place, where nothing really disturbs the peace except the postman, the parking ticket patrol, the waste disposal truck, the delivery lorry to the tearoom in the old mill, the 10,000 tourists who pass every summer on their way to explore the Rushing Wood, as well as all the people who go walking, running, cycling and exercising dogs every day, the sound of car alarms is seldom heard there. Mr Ferraby had never even heard his car's alarm before. He burst out of his house, ready to rescue his beloved machine. Thieves, bandits and vandals were rarely seen on Woodside Terrace but now Mr Ferraby imagined a horde of them attacking Liebling Trudi. (This was his secret name for his car, because she was so German, so glossy and so sleek.)

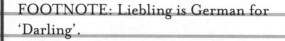

FOOTNOTE: Liebling is German for 'Darling'.

Mr Ferraby believed he was going to have to fight about ten vandals and/or bandits, certainly two or three. He was determined to defend Liebling Trudi to the last. His chances of victory were non-existent, he knew, and it was a pity he must die now, in the prime of his late middle age, but if his time had come he was ready. His doomed last stand would make Trudi proud of him, and Mrs Ferraby too.

Braced for a death-struggle with all the crazy-faced cohorts of hell, Mr Ferraby was entirely unprepared for the sight of Aubrey, standing in the driving seat of his father's car – the nose of which was rammed into the back of Liebling Trudi – gripping the wheel with both hands and smiling a reassuring smile. 'You little vandal bandit!' Mr Ferraby cried.

As soon as she heard Trudi's alarm Suzanne felt a familiar conviction: her son was in action somewhere nearby. Suzanne could move with great speed when she wanted to: she was out of the garden and down to the lane so quickly that the boy believed she must have jumped over the house. 'Aubrey! Aubrey?' she called, as she flew towards the noise.

On her arrival, Aubrey gave her his reassuring smile too.

Jim woke and stuck his head out of the attic window as the appalling noise of mechanical panic filled the afternoon with honk-wailing.

'Aubrey?' he called. 'Is that you?'

Suzanne lifted the little boy out of the car and Aubrey gave his father a champion's grin – such a radiant, triumphant smile that you would have thought crashing the cars was exactly what everyone had been hoping he would do, and now they were going to give him a medal for it. His father could not help himself. He laughed.

Mr Ferraby switched off Liebling Trudi's

alarm and looked up at his laughing neighbour with the expression of a man whose dentist's drilling hand has just slipped.

'Sorry, sorry, Mr Ferraby,' said Aubrey's father, 'Is there much damage? I'm coming down...'

'Your car has a great alarm, Mr Ferraby!' said Aubrey, admiringly, but his compliment was lost under the many apologies his mother was making, and the telling-off she was giving him at the same time.

'Did you just jump over the house, Mum?' he asked her, but she did not seem to hear. She was very busy with Mr Ferraby.

Mr Ferraby did not go bright red and roar, 'If you can't control that child I am going to eat him!' which part of him longed to roar – the same part which wanted to throw his hat on the ground and stamp on it until he felt better. He was a good man, and besides, he was not wearing a hat.

'The boy's alright, is he?' he asked, with wonderful courtesy.

'He is,' Suzanne said. 'And he's never going to do anything like that again. Apologise to Mr Ferraby, Aubrey!'

'Sorry Mr Ferraby,' said Aubrey. 'I tried to miss.'

'Doesn't look like there's much harm done,' Mr Ferraby said, with immense self-control. He could see a blistering big dent in Liebling Trudi's back bumper.

'Very sorry, Mr Ferraby,' Suzanne said, fiercely. 'And I'll never do anything so stupid again.'

'Very sorry Mr Ferraby,' Aubrey said. 'I've never done anything so stupid again.'

'Alright,' said Mr Ferraby, quietly. 'No one's hurt, that's the main thing.' He retreated into his house, where Mrs Ferraby was making a pot of tea. He gave her a strained smile. 'That was Aubrey,' he told her, 'smashing up the car.'

Jim and Suzanne's joint lecture about The Car Incident seemed to work. They were horrified (once Jim had stopped laughing) about the damage Aubrey could have caused, and they blamed themselves for leaving the key where he could reach it. As it turned out, hitting Trudi was the best thing Aubrey could have done. Had he missed her, and set off in a car which he had no way of controlling... Suzanne said she, 'shuddered to think of the consequences'.

Aubrey said he would have used the handbrake and Jim said actually the lane levelled out and he wouldn't have got far, but Suzanne said she was not interested in their theories: what was dangerous, illegal and wrong would always be dangerous, illegal and wrong. Jim and Aubrey had to agree with that.

Of course Aubrey still ignored his parents' instructions when it came to flooding the bathroom, raiding the fridge, skiing down the stairs (which came much closer to killing him than driving the car), wearing the cat like a bearskin hat, setting water traps for Jim and riding his bicycle backwards down the steep bit of the garden. (He only needed three stitches after that, which Suzanne did for him.) But he was careful not to pull anything too stylish, dramatic or dangerous, because he loved his parents and did not want to worry them.

For the next few years the boy went to school, read books, messed about, played games with his friends, loved the holidays, and grew. But then the horrendous spell came over his father and everything began to change.

CHAPTER 2
The Spell

'What's up with Dad?' Aubrey asked his mother, as they did the shopping one rainy Saturday afternoon. 'His face is like a sinking moon.'

'He's just a bit worried,' Suzanne said. 'He could do with some cheering up.'

'What's he worried about?'

Suzanne shook her head. 'He's not really sure. He's not sleeping much at night.'

'Is that why he's sleeping today?'

'Yes. We need to make sure he eats well, sleeps and takes lots of exercise – so if he asks you to go for a walk, do go. And if he doesn't, you ask him, would you darling? It's just what he needs.'

'Sure,' said Aubrey.

Suzanne was a nurse, a very good one, and what she said was true. When people are

worried, food, sleep, exercise and kindness
are exactly what they need. But Suzanne
could not know that her husband was
falling under a spell, an horrendous spell
of tremendous strength and power. Aubrey,
Suzanne and Jim all knew something was
wrong, but they had no idea what it was.

'OK Dad?'

Aubrey and Jim were walking to school.
Normally Jim would be looking at the trees,
at the clouds, at the birds and at Aubrey,
and chatting away about everything. Jim
was the sort of English teacher whose jacket
is sometimes a bit scruffy, whose shirts are
old and comfortable rather than sharp and
new, whose hair occasionally looks more
happy than neat, and who loves telling
stories. He was not a man to miss anything
interesting, and everything was interesting
to him normally.

But this morning he was looking at his
feet, as though all he wanted to do was

watch his shoes walking down the lane.

'Hm? Oh, yes. Fine.'

'You don't look that fine,' said Aubrey.

'Don't I?'

'You look like a man wearing a heavy hat.'

Jim smiled and squeezed his shoulder.

'That's exactly right,' he said. 'That is how

I feel. Like a man wearing a heavy hat.
I'm sure it'll pass – it's probably just the
summer ending, and going back to work.'

'But you love work! You love teaching!'

Jim sighed. 'I do, normally. It's just this
heavy hat.'

On the way back from school, as they
walked up the lane, Aubrey took a long look
at Jim. His father's face was pale and tense.
His gaze seemed empty. It was as though
his eyes stared into his own mind and saw
only sad thoughts there.

'How's the heavy hat, Dad?' Aubrey asked
quietly.

Jim looked down at him and swallowed.
Aubrey could see his father struggling
with what to say next.

'It's still there,' he said, huskily. 'And
there's something else.'

'What?'

'There's a feeling in my stomach.'

'What's it like?'

'It's like ... you mustn't worry, Aubrey Boy. It's just a feeling. Feelings pass, you know?'

'I know!' Aubrey exclaimed. 'But what does it feel like?'

'It's like a hairy worm,' his father said quietly, and as he said it he looked frightened.

The next morning, and the morning after that, Suzanne drove Aubrey to school.

'Dad's still not feeling well,' she said. 'He's having another day in bed.'

(Aubrey had expected this. He had overheard Suzanne asking Jim how he felt that morning. Jim said he felt 'Horrendous.')

'Is it the hairy worm and the heavy hat?'

She nodded. 'Yes. And the panicked bird.'

'What bird?'

'He says it feels as though he has a

panicked bird in his chest, trying to get out.'

'Is that why he feels horrendous?'

'Yes darling, that's right.'

Aubrey took a deep breath. 'So – can you cure him, Mum?

He knew his mother could cure pretty well anything. He watched her face, hoping for her reassuring smile. It was such a beautiful, calming smile that Suzanne's patients felt better just for seeing it. But that smile did not come. Instead, her mouth bent into a frown, and her head gave a slow half-shake.

'It's very difficult,' she said. 'If he had a germ or a virus or a wound or a disease I could help him. But it isn't any of those. We just have to look after him, and be very gentle with him until he comes out of it. And we have to be cheery and optimistic, OK?'

'OK!' said Aubrey, with a cheerfulness he did not really feel.

'Good boy!' said his mother. 'Such a good

boy! You are wonderful at being cheerful and optimistic!'

After school the first thing Aubrey did was run upstairs to see his father. He found Jim out of bed, half dressed, wearing old trousers, one of his best shirts, and one sock.

'Hello, Aubrey Boy!' His father's lips made a shape which looked as though it was trying very hard to be a smile.

'Hullo Dad. Are you feeling better?'

'Sort of,' his father said. 'I can't seem to decide what to wear.'

'Are you going out?'

'No, just coming down to make supper. I think. Or is your mother making it?'

And that was the start of the indecisions.

Over the next few days Jim made indecision after indecision.

If you asked him whether he wanted tea or coffee he could not tell you. It was as though he made haphazard guesses instead.

He repeated the question, 'Tea? Or coffee?' as though he'd never had the choice before. Then he came out with 'Tea! Please! If you're having some? Or coffee?'

Which was not very helpful. And poor Jim knew it.

'Dad?'
'Yes?'
'Would you rather play in the garden or walk in the wood?'

Jim looked agonised. Different expressions ran over his face, as if he wanted to play in the garden and walk in the wood at the same time, and at the same time did not want to walk in the wood or play in the garden at all, but felt that he ought to do one of them because Aubrey wanted to, and so was trying to work out which Aubrey would like most – when all Aubrey had asked him was which one he wanted to do!

Asking Jim what he wanted for supper, lunch or breakfast was a great mistake.

He simply had no idea. When he dressed he chose his clothes strangely and looked miserable in them. He stayed in bed a great deal, curled up as though he was cold. He said sorry a lot, apologising for being tired, for being sad, for being lost. But no matter how many times you said it was fine, he didn't have to say sorry, Jim kept seeming sorrier and sorrier and sadder and sadder.

Soon Jim's pale face and wobbly eyes made him look like a ghost who has spooked himself in a mirror. He took a second week off work, but instead of recovering his bounce he seemed to lose every last scrap of it. His zip was gone; there was no sign of his zing. You would have thought he had never had a spring in his step. Sometimes he seemed so wispy he might have been made of mist. Suzanne took him to the doctor, of course. The doctor said there was nothing physically wrong with him. The problem was in his thoughts.

'He's unhappy but he doesn't know why. You could call it the blues, or the glums,' Suzanne explained to Aubrey. 'It happens to lots of people. They just feel very sad. But they get better. He'll get better if we look after him: he needs food and rest and love.'

Aubrey nodded but he was not really listening to this stuff about blue gums. His father's gums weren't blue, they were pink. He was quite surprised his mother had missed that, but he was too busy to worry about it. He was working out what to do about the horrendous spell.

CHAPTER 3
How Do You Break a Spell?

First he looked up 'Horrendous Spell' on the internet. He found lots of pages about spelling 'horrendous' (but he could do that) and pages about why people's spelling is horrendous (ignorance, carelessness or disability, apparently) and he found pages on various horrendous spells you could use in games, like Horrendous Shout, which knocks monsters back a bit and stops them hitting you, and Horrendous Desiccation which sounded fantastic. Aubrey read the description: 'Everything within 300 feet of the spell-caster becomes withered and desiccated.'

He looked up 'desiccated'. It means dried out: a desiccated plant is a plant that has died for lack of water.

Aubrey thought about learning Horrendous
Desiccation. It would be tremendous to
see it in action! But even watching his
son desiccate a circle of wood 600 feet in
diameter probably wouldn't cheer Jim up all
that much. Also, Aubrey had private reasons
for not wanting to upset Rushing Wood.

'Concentrate!' Aubrey told himself. 'Stick
to saving Dad. You can always learn
Horrendous Desiccation when he's better.
Now, how are we going to do this?'

Aubrey narrowed his eyes and thought
hard. Supposing we go about it the other
way, he thought. Supposing I look up his
symptoms on the net, then it can tell me
what's wrong with him, then I can look up
what to do. How simple everything is with
the net! He found a symptom checker very
easily. It asked a lot of questions.

'Where are you?' demanded the
symptom checker.

'In the attic,' Aubrey typed into the box.

'Postcode not recognised,' replied the symptom checker. 'This advice is for people in the UK only.'

'MUM! WHAT'S OUR POSTCODE?'
'HX10 8AJ!' Suzanne shouted.
Aubrey typed it in.

'How old are you?' asked the checker. 'Please confirm you are being supervised by an adult.'

Aubrey wanted to type 'Sort of!' but there wasn't a box for it. You either had to click Yes or No.

He read the instruction again. Please confirm you are being supervised – OK, he thought, if that's what you want. Since you can't confirm something by denying it, and since the symptom checker was asking him to confirm something, he clicked Yes.

Now the questions came like a swarm of midges.

Was the sick person's tongue swelling up? Could he breathe? Was it possible to wake him up? Were the whites of his eyes yellow? Was he drowsy? Were there little red pin-pricks on his skin? Were his feet cold? Did he go to the loo a lot? Did he have diabetes? Was he weak, dizzy or lightheaded? Did he have a rash? Had he been bitten or stung? Did he have a temperature? Was his skin cold or clammy?

Answering these questions meant taking the computer down to his parents' room and giving Jim a thorough check-up before clicking Yes or No to each question.

'What are you up to, Aubrey Boy?' his father asked, as Aubrey peered at Jim's eyeballs, squeezed his tongue, felt his feet and looked for rashes.

'Have you been bitten? Do you feel drowsy?' Aubrey demanded.

'No – well, not really. What's biting you?'

'Have you got diabetes?' Aubrey asked.

'No! Well, I don't think so. The doctor didn't mention it. Why?'

'What does clammy mean?'

'Sort of damp and a bit sticky. Cold and wet but not that cold and – not that wet,' Jim said, looking a bit embarrassed. 'Dampish...'

'It's OK, you're not,' Aubrey said. 'That's strange.'

'Why? Should I be clammy?'

'I'm finding out what's wrong with you so that we can cure it,' Aubrey said. 'Just keep quiet please. Keep calm. Eat something. Rest.'

'Oh my wonderful boy!' Jim cried, sweeping Aubrey up in a hug. His arms felt thin and bony.

'My wonderful boy!' he exclaimed again, and he had tears in his eye.

'Why are you crying, Dad?'

'I'm not! You shouldn't be worried – and it's all my fault! I love you so much, and I'm so sorry I'm depressed, and not a happy Dad, not a sparky Dad – I'm so sorry!'

'You ARE!' Aubrey said, 'Normally you are sparky!'

His father put him down and Aubrey was about to spin back to the computer but at that moment his mother called him to tea. Jim said he would have his later. Jim's meal times had all moved later.

Aubrey and his mum ate fish pie. It was delicious, with a creamy sauce lathered all over golden potato and lumps of juicy fish. Even so, Suzanne almost spat fish across the kitchen when Aubrey said, 'Mum, has Dad gone bats?'

'No!' she said. 'Why do you ask?'

'He was almost crying when he said he was sorry he wasn't sparky.'

'Oh! That's OK,' Suzanne said, smiling

seriously. 'He's a very loving man and it makes him sad not to be able to be funny and fun for you.'

'When will he be better, Mum?'

Suzanne put down her knife and fork.

'The fact is darling, we don't know. It could last a week, it could last a month, or even more. We just can't tell. It's a strange thing, this feeling of sadness. I haven't had much experience of it and nor has he. But I'd be surprised if he doesn't start bobbing back up soon. I think he was just over-tired.'

'So he's depressed?'

'Yes – it just means he's very sad, and he can't make himself happy in the normal ways.'

Hmm, thought Aubrey, he can't make himself happy in the normal ways. That means we have to go beyond the normal.

CHAPTER 4
The Secret

You have guessed Aubrey is the sort of child who has secrets. He does not think of them as secrets, exactly. Like many children, he thinks of them as his private business. Secrets are like baby dragons. They are fine as long as they are happy, playful little creatures (I have access to some chocolate no one knows about) and not so fine if they grow into smouldering beasts (I accidentally killed next door's rabbit during catapult practice). Private business is quite different. Everyone has a right to that.

Listening to his mother, and thinking about Jim's trouble, Aubrey began to suspect that the answer to his father's problem might lie somewhere in this private, secret world.

We are therefore about to enter the treasury of Aubrey's Private Life. We are not going to poke around in here, of course, but we are going to be allowed into one or two secrets: the one or two which made all the difference to this story.

So, here we go.

Aubrey had secret adventures in Rushing Wood at night. He called it Night Venturing. Sometimes, when the moon was high and full, when glades of silver beams glowed between the tree trunks, and sometimes, when the moon struggled to see through flying clouds and the wood rustled and the wind dashed through the sky in a hurry to get home – sometimes, on certain nights, after Suzanne had kissed him and Jim had read him a story and turned off the light, Aubrey went Night Venturing.

His body lay warm under the covers, but in his mind he got up and pushed the window open ever so quietly, and clambered out.

There was an old iron drainpipe next to his window which was very easy to climb. When he went on these adventures Aubrey could even feel the cold smoothness of the pipe in his palms, and his toes finding grip in the rough stone wall as he lowered himself down to the ground. Up to the top of the garden he went, damp leaves beneath his feet, and over the fence, and into Rushing Wood.

Rushing Wood! Was there ever such a place at night? The wood was ghostly silver. The wood was a hush of whispers. The wood had shadows which brushed your legs like cats, and secrets as deep as caves. The wood was tangled with all the wisdom of its ancient trees, and alive with a million creatures. It was a night city of mice and bugs and owls and voles. It was a metropolis of foxes, pine martens, slugs and rabbits, of caterpillars, badgers and wild runaway sheep – and that was if you only believed in the everyday!

If you thought all of life begins with

breakfast and ends with a snore, every day, everywhere, for all time...

Aubrey did not believe that for a minute. You did not have to have much imagination, he thought, to feel that there were great stags in the wood too, noble deer whose ancestors had faced down the hunting dogs of kings. And if there were stags there were certainly boar, with tusks so sharp they could shred armour and gore giants. And if there were boar there must be little boar piglets, with pelts like striped pyjamas.

He encountered such creatures on his Night Ventures, when he sent himself out in his imagination from deep within the snuggled comfort of his bed. Aubrey sometimes fell asleep playing Catch Fish! with the otters in the brook, or wrestling with pine martens – the pine martens loved to playfight as much as Aubrey did. As he fell into sleep within sleep he travelled in dreams within dreams to the Enchanted Mountains, where wolves glide under

giant fir trees and bears teach their cubs to
toboggan by the light of the stars.

And never in any of his deepest dreams,
never in any wish or fantasy, did Aubrey
think he would have to venture out into

the waiting, listening darkness of the night
when he was wide awake, in reality.

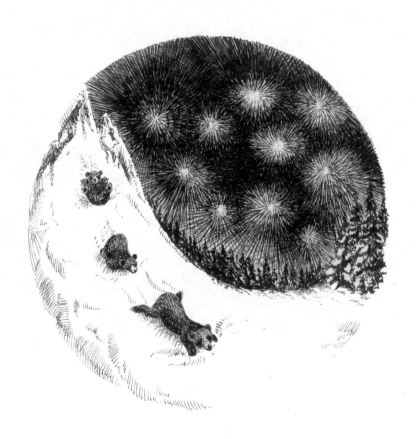

CHAPTER 5
The Owl

Aubrey was lying in bed that night, after the fish pie supper, and a game of cards with his mother, and a bath, and a few pages of his favourite story, which was the tale of Perseus cutting the Gorgon's head off. Aubrey loved to read and re-read that story in *Greek Gods, Myths and Monsters*. Now it was late; he had heard his parents going to bed. The house had fallen silent. As he lay there he was thinking. His thoughts went like this.

'How do you solve a problem that won't be solved in the normal ways?'

'You need wise advice.'

'Yes! Someone wise. Someone very wise! Who is wise? Who is the wisest person in the world?'

'Uuum ... if only I could look it up...'

'Think!'

'Gandalf?'

'He's a fictional character.'

'Merlin, then.'

'Maybe. He's a mythical character and myths are partly true.'

'Where can I find him?'

'I don't know.'

'Rats.'

'If only I could look up "the wisest person who I can actually find"...'

'You could, if you had the computer.'

'Ah!'

'Computer, computer, bright and small, Who's the wisest of us all?'

He was not allowed to have the computer in his bedroom after bedtime, but his rhyme made him smile.

Then he remembered something and grabbed for the light switch. There on the carpet, where he had left it, was *Greek Gods, Myths and Monsters*. Normally it

looked
like any
other good
book – a pretty
cover, with a
dramatic picture (this one showed Odysseus
and his crew fighting Polyphemus, the
Cyclops) and the title.

But now the book's colours were especially
bright. The single eye of the Cyclops glowed
so red it might have been looking at Aubrey
and actually seeing him.

Don't be silly, Aubrey told himself. A book is a book. It's just my eyes adjusting back from dark to light. He grabbed *Greek Gods, Myths and Monsters* and opened it. He had a peculiar feeling that there was something going on between the book, whose pages his fingers were riffling through even now, the thoughts in his head, and the problem that could not be solved in normal ways.

'There!' he said, aloud. And there she was, in the story of Perseus. The wisest person in all creation: Pallas Athene! Athene who helped Perseus in his quest to kill the terrible Medusa, whose gaze turned people to stone. Athene, Goddess of Wisdom, and many other virtues, including Civilisation, Inspiration, Justice and Courage (with a line-up like that you can see why the Ancient Greeks named their greatest city Athens).

Athene does not live in Athens, Aubrey read. Her home address is Mount Olympus,

Macedonia and Thessaly, Greece.

Aubrey slid out of bed and pulled his *Atlas of the World* from his bookshelf.

'Right,' he said to himself, after studying the maps for a minute or two. 'Tricky.'

Basically, Aubrey saw, the journey from Woodside Terrace to Mount Olympus involved going to London, crossing to France and taking a route through Belgium, Germany, Austria, Hungary, Serbia and Macedonia down to northern Greece. It looked about 2000 miles. Admittedly, it had been a few years since he last tried to make a serious expedition without telling his parents, but although he was sure he could do better on a second attempt (he would

FOOTNOTE: Athene helped Perseus get hold of an eye which could see around corners, and gave him a polished shield. When he found Medusa Perseus hid, watched her with the eye, and when her reflection in the polished shield told him she was close enough – swap! He cut off her head.

certainly miss Liebling Trudi this time)
a secret 2000-mile trip to Greece would
probably put a strain on the family.

He imagined it was breakfast time.

His mother has gone downstairs to make
tea. She sees a note on the kitchen table.
She picks it up.

Dear Mum and Dad, I have just popped over
to Greece for a few days to see someone.
Don't worry I have the Atlas. Should be
back soon and it's a straight road love you
Aubrey xxx
ps I borrowed the car
ppps don't worry, really

Perhaps not, Aubrey concluded.

He shut the Atlas. He felt a bit glum. It
was such a good idea! Athene was the right
person! But he could not get to her place,
and so he was still stuck, and his father
too. He climbed back into bed. He picked
up *Greek Gods, Myths and Monsters* again,

without thinking about it, and turned over the Athene page. And there it was, looking at him with huge, wise eyes.

The answer.

'Whoo hooo!' cried Aubrey, without thinking about it.

From outside the window, an owl answered.

'Hooo-Woo!' it said.

Aubrey jumped in surprise.

The picture he was looking at was a picture of an owl. (Wherever you find Athene you will always find an owl. It is Athene's bird, the symbol of wisdom, which is why you find so many of them lurking around schools and libraries.)

'Weird!' said Aubrey, boldly, aloud, though his heart was beating rather fast. 'Owls don't talk to people!'

There was a distinct pause, in which the world seemed to go very quiet.

And the owl answered.

'We-doo-too!' it said.

Well, Aubrey thinks, this is different. He opens his bedroom window to a warm and hazy autumn night. The moon is a coppery crescent, cushioned on fine cloud. Nothing moves in the garden. The trees at the edge of the wood are still.

But now something shifts there, a little shape of shadow. Even as he watches, the shape swoops down the garden in an easy glide. So silent is its flight that Aubrey feels no alarm at all as it falls quickly towards him, flares out its wings and lands, with the merest brush of feathers, on his windowsill.

Aubrey's breath stops in his chest. An owl – a wild owl – just there! If he moves his hand he will touch it. He could stroke the tawny feathers of the bird's magnificent head.

'Please do, if you want to,' the bird says. 'It is perfectly good manners among owls.'

Aubrey is so doubly surprised that the surprises cancel one another out, leaving him surprisingly cool. Though he hears the words clearly, the owl's beak does not move. Its words arrive in Aubrey's head complete, audible but unspoken.

Telepathic owl, Aubrey thinks.

He stretches out his hand.

The owl's expression comes from the deep gaze of dark eyes, set in double circles of delicate feathers. It makes the owl look like a little professor. But the words Aubrey heard were gentle and encouraging, so he dares.

He strokes the owl's head. The plumage is warm, the feathers rounded tight together. The owl rolls its head against the palm of his hand like a cat.

'You read my mind,' Aubrey whispers.

'Assuredly!' the owl replies, in his thoughts. 'All animals and birds do likewise, insects too. Fish are the exception because thoughts cannot pass through water. Once you fish them out they can hear what you have in mind – though it tends to be pretty obvious by then.'

'Poor fish!'

'Oh they have a marvellous time when they're not being eaten,' says the owl. 'I promise you, fish have a tremendously entertaining existence compared to most organisms. They spend half their lives in fits of giggles. Are you ready? You might need your dressing gown. And slippers.'

'Ready for what?'

'Night Venturing?'

'Hang on!' Aubrey hisses. 'I don't know what sort of dream this is, telepathic owls and giggling fish, but I like to go Night Venturing from my bed and in my head, so...'

At this point our whole story hangs in the balance. Aubrey even takes hold of the curtains: he is about to shut them on this unlikely and demanding bird and go back to bed. He hesitates.

The owl opens his dark eyes amazingly wide and hoots.

'HOO! You're dreaming, are you? Then I must be too! Are you by any chance dreaming about an owl who is dreaming about a boy who is dreaming about an owl who wants to help a boy who wants to help his father who is in all sorts of trouble? You are? WOO! So you are the boy, I am the owl – or is it the other way round?' (The owl looks confused for a second.) 'Anyway, I am in your dream, you are in mine, and that, my rambunctious friend, is what we in the business call LIFE! My name is Augustus, by the way – Augustus Howell-Brown Bachelor of Arts Master of Arts Master of Philosophy Doctor of Philosophy milk no sugar if only we had time for tea. Augustus for short. What a pleasure to meet you. Shall we go?'

Aubrey sways, smiling.

'How do you know me, Augustus?'

'We creatures have learned to listen to humans carefully. We have to. Thanks to your Night Venturing the whole wood knows you. And we like you, and your wonderful mother, and poor Jim. So – dressing gown – slippers – *yallah!*

Augustus gives Aubrey a huge, encouraging blink.

FOOTNOTE: Oh-ho, you may be thinking, a story with talking animals in it. How anthropomorphic. Anthropomorphic is a beautiful word, from the Greek words anthropos (human) and morphe (shape). It means making animals look and sound like people. And not just animals – it could be gods, clouds, cars (like Liebling Trudi) – anything you please.

However, as you will see, the philosophy of this story is closer to animism. Animism is one of our oldest ideas. Animism says that humans are not the centre of the universe, because everything in nature has a soul or a spirit, and that plants and rivers and owls have their own existences in the same way you do. (This is why you sometimes overhear people like Suzanne saying things like 'Hello, woodpigeon!')

CHAPTER 6

Unkillable Monster, Impossible Quest

'Was that a spell?' Aubrey asks.

'No-o!' Augustus hoots, 'That was "Let's go!" in Arabic.'

'Show-off!'

'My choice of habitation happens to be a British wood,' Augustus says, with dignity. 'It does not mean I am stuck in the mud.'

They are walking through the wood. Aubrey has on his dressing gown and slippers. Augustus sits on his shoulder. Because Augustus is able to see their path between the stumps and roots a hundred times more clearly than Aubrey can, the owl directs the boy right or left.

'Augustus, you won't fly off and leave me, will you?'

'You would be
discomforted to find
yourself all alone in the Great
Wood in the middle of the night in
total darkness, in dressing gown and
slippers, when no one knows you are
out here, and you are unsure of the way
back?'

'I could find my way back!' Aubrey
whispers. (The darkness and the
presence of the great trees make him
want to whisper.)

'Good lad,' Augustus replies, and
Aubrey can hear an owlish smile in the
words, as they form in his head. 'Don't
worry. You are as safe in this wood as
you are in your own bed, more or less.'

'I like the "more",' Aubrey mutters.

He knows the leaves have turned to all
the colours of a slow fire, he can smell
a lot of them, but most have not yet
fallen, so under the canopy the night is

deeply dark. Occasionally he glimpses the crescent moon high up. He can only make out the vaguest outlines of the individual trees. They seem to stand all around him like the legs of huge beasts.

'Turn right up here,' Augustus tells him. 'We follow this path to the top. Do you know where you are?'

'Roughly...'

'There's a clearing at the top of this bank, between an oak tree, an ash tree and a beech tree. It's a meeting place.'

'Are we meeting someone?'

'You were thinking about wisdom, I believe.'

'Yes,' Aubrey puffs, as he stumbles up the path. It is quite steep. 'And here you are, Augustus! Wisely riding on my shoulder, hitching a lift home, saving yourself the effort of walking, or flying...'

'Oh,' Augustus says, 'I'm just a messenger really. The wise one is waiting at the top.'

'Who's that?'

'She is Athene Noctua. Whom I believe you were hoping to meet?'

'The goddess Athene! She's come all the way from Greece?'

'Not the woman!' Augustus laughs. 'Athene Noctua – the owl!'

'An owl, like you?'

Aubrey makes sure he doesn't sound disappointed. Augustus is a very fine owl, after all.

'An owl,' Augustus confirms, 'but not like me. I am a Tawny Owl, Strix aluco. One does not wish to be immodest, but the plain fact is, in the lottery of life I am extremely fortunate. But Athene Noctua! She is … well, she is another order of fowl altogether. Companion of Pallas Athene herself! It's not so much a question of respect as due reverence.'

'Right. Phee-ew!' blows Aubrey, as the steep path tops the bank and the trees drop back, and there is the clearing, soft and dim as a dream within a dream in the moonlight.

'I will leave you here,' Augustus says, softly. 'Don't worry, Athene will look after you.'

Before Aubrey can say anything there is a single beat of silent wings and Augustus vanishes into the dark.

Aubrey stands alone on the edge of the clearing. When an owl says it's not going to leave you... Aubrey thinks – or did he actually say that?

'Welcome!' says a voice, which seems to come from below his right knee. Aubrey jumps like a rabbit.

Athene Noctua is perched on an anthill.

The anthill is two feet high. Athene Noctua is not much taller than a coffee mug. She really is a tiny owl, but her bright yellow eyes are huge.

'Do sit!'

Her voice is snappy and quick but not unfriendly.

'Don't worry, the ants are all asleep. You won't be stung.'

'We're not all asleep,' pipes a tiny voice from the hill, quite distinctly. 'Some of us are trying to sleep.'

Athene Noctua laughs. Aubrey sits. I'm dreaming, the boy thinks, but it's a good one!

'So. You are Aubrey Rambunctious Wolf.'

'I'm who?'

'It's your Wild Name. It's how we think of you. And your father is in the grip of the Terrible Yoot, and you want to help.'

'The Terrible what?'

'The YOOT. Think of it as a monster which can't be killed.'

Aubrey feels fear, something like his father's hairy worm, small but definitely there, stirring in his stomach.

'Can't be killed?' he repeats.

In every myth and legend, every story he has ever read, the monster can always be killed, somehow.

Athene Noctua stares hard at him. 'You can fight the Yoot,' she says. 'You can run away from the Yoot, you can try hiding from the Yoot, you can negotiate with the Yoot – people have been known to befriend it, too – but you cannot kill it.'

'Why is it picking on my dad?'

'Your father is unlucky. He is not alone – the Yoot picks on most people – but some people, about one person in every ten, are more vulnerable than others. The majority are women, and it's getting to more people every year. More children too.'

Aubrey now feels very angry. Whoever or whatever this thing is, someone needs to stand up to it!

'How can I beat this Yoot?' he demands. Athene Noctua hops closer to Aubrey. The bird's huge yellow eyes glare up at his and do not blink. Meeting her gaze is like staring into swirls of antique power. These dark pupils in their blazing irises have watched the shaping and changing of the world. The boy is almost hypnotised. 'Don't blink,' he tells himself, not knowing quite why. Suddenly the owl's pupils dilate, the black holes widening, and Athene Noctua smiles.

'Understand this,' she says. 'You are undertaking a quest with only one

FOOTNOTE: An owl's smile is felt, not seen. The birds smile by sending out a warm pulse of friendship. It's difficult to explain but impossible to mistake when you feel it. The next time you hear an owl, send it a mental message of friendship and I guarantee you'll get one back. No owl ever fails to respond.

certainty: you cannot simply succeed. The Yoot will still be there at the end. You may help your father but you might not. You may put yourself in great danger. There is every chance that forgetting the Yoot – and me, and Augustus – and going back to your normal life will have exactly the same result: your father will get better, slowly, or he will stay the same, or he will get worse. Tell me you understand.'

'I understand,' says Aubrey. But he thinks, *this Yoot is not going to get away as easily as that...*

Athene Noctua continues: 'The best thing might be for the doctors to give him some pills to help put the Yoot out of his mind. Your assistance, however determined and rambunctious, may not be what he needs.'

Aubrey thinks for a moment, then he leans forward too, so that his nose is only a few centimetres from Athene's beak.

'Athene,' Aubrey says, very clearly, 'tell

me where I can find this thing which goes
around terrorising one person in ten and
picks on women and children and which is
getting stronger every year and which is
attacking my father every day and every
night. I'm going to give it a battle it will
never forget. By the time I've finished, this
Yoot is going to be begging me for its head!'

   Athene Noctua's eyes blaze gold and she
cries 'Keeey-WIICK!'

'I knew it!' she laughs, 'That is exactly what Perseus said when I warned him about the Medusa. So. You don't just go charging off at the Yoot. Practice and preparation first.'

'What – like those bits in films where the hero goes running and does press-ups?' Aubrey says, disappointed. 'Really?'

'Not you,' Athene snaps, 'your father. To have any chance against the Yoot we'll need to build Jim up. Your mother is quite right, of course – he needs sleep, food, especially oily fish, rest, exercise, practical work (like gardening) and lots of positive thinking.'

'But he's been resting and eating and it's not working!' Aubrey objects, 'He's getting worse!'

'Just because it hasn't worked yet does not mean it won't,' Athene says, gently. 'And besides, you haven't had our help before.'

'Whose help?'

'We, the Creatures,' Athene Noctua says, simply. 'How quickly you humans forget where you come from, and who your best friends are. Have you ever seen people and animals working together?'

Aubrey thinks.

'Sheepdogs?'

'Exactly,' says Athene. 'In this case, Jim is the sheep.'

CHAPTER 7

Surprising Events at Woodside Terrace

On an October day in the half-term holiday when the sun was warm and the air so clear that every leaf and blade of grass seemed to tremble in the beauty of its being, and you could see spider webs shining like threads of spun light, Mr Ferraby was looking out of the window at his garden. It ran up the hill to the edge of the wood. Mr Ferraby was thinking how lovely it was to be alive on such a perfect autumn morning when his eye caught a movement at the edge of the wood.

Aubrey was standing there talking to a fence post. Well, thought Mr Ferraby, he is an unusual child.

Then the top of the fence post moved. Mr Ferraby reached for his glasses. He put them on and looked again. Ah! There was a squirrel at the top of the post. Huh? Aubrey appeared to be in conversation with it.

Mr Ferraby watched for some time. He could see Aubrey's mouth moving as he talked to the creature. He could see the squirrel's tail switching, and its head bobbing, as if it understood what the boy was saying. There were also long pauses, in which Aubrey seemed to listen and the squirrel twitched, jumped and ducked about on the top of the post. Then the squirrel bobbed and disappeared.

'I just saw Aubrey talking to a squirrel,' Mr Ferraby told his wife. 'Funny thing. It was as though the squirrel was talking back.'

Mrs Ferraby raised her eyebrows. She did not look convinced.

Athene had not told Aubrey where or when the Creatures would contact him. All she said was, 'Don't get stuck indoors. Someone will find you.'

So that morning Aubrey went out and wondered if the bees would talk to him, or if the buzzard turning circles above the trees had something to say. But the bees just buzzed and the buzzard soared away.

He said 'Hello!' to a frog in the pond. The frog looked startled and ducked under water. Aubrey was feeling a bit foolish when there was a burst of movement in the bushes like a small explosion. With a scrabble of claws a grey squirrel raced up the fence and stopped on top of the post, flicking her beautiful tail.

'YO BREE!'

'Whoa! Hello, Squirrel,' said Aubrey, surprised that Athene should have sent someone who looked so young and playful to help him battle the Terrible Yoot.

'Hey Bree! I'm Hoppy. How's it? You look stressed. What's up?'

'I...'

'Have a sad Dad? I know! And – what?'

'Well...'

'How can I help you help him help himself, right? So, how can I?'

Hoppy was giving him such a toothy grin it was difficult not to smile.

'I don't know,' Aubrey said. 'How can you?'

'Do I look happy, Bree?'

'Yes! You do look hoppy, Happy. I mean the other way round. I've never seen a squirrel look sad. Why is that?'

'Secret,' Hoppy said, peeling a bit of bark off the post and flicking it at him. 'Bad stuff can happen to squirrels, same as anyone – airguns, hate them, cars, hate them, goshawks – brrr! We get cold, wet, ill, all that, but we basically stay happy. Amazing!'

'How do you do it?'

'Oh, Bree! It's so easy! Listen, you've never run up a tree really fast, have you? But you must have climbed them. Best feeling in the world, right? And when we learn to climb we also learn to fall. That's a biggie. Go away gravity, go away planet – that really doesn't work when you're plunging towards it face first. Point is, you're not trying to fend the ground off! You're trying to make friends with it at speed. So you go very floppy and you roll like hell, that's the trick. And you laugh. Once you can fall and climb, which is easy when you've got *these* babies.' (The squirrel flourished her right paw, and its small sharp claws.) 'Then you can start sprinting on air. And fly-jumping!'

As she spoke Hoppy acted out what she was describing, jumping on the spot, going floppy, and now, tensing like a small cannonball.

'What you do is, you gather yourself up, tense your muscles – say you're about thirty feet up – and you just fill your eyes with all the trees and leaves and branches ahead of you, and you sort of pick an aiming point – like a good oak or big pine that sticks up and you say to yourself, I am going to get there SO fast – and you take three deep breaths, and you count, one, two, three, GO!'

Hoppy leapt into the air and came back down on top of the post.

'You take off like a goshawk is after you
and you rip along the first branch and when
it runs out you fling yourself at the next
one and hurl yourself off that and then you
hit whatever you can catch and the idea is
to go faster all the time and sometimes you
just run out of tree and you shriek! Because
you're in terror and you're laughing too and
Wheeee! You jump then like you wouldn't
believe, you really LEAP! And you have to
think I've got Flying Squirrel in me! I'm a

jet! And you stick
your tail way out
and use it like a kind of
wing, it balances you, and you
steer with it too and now all the
leaves and twigs are just blurring past
you, that's what we call the Green Rush. And
then – then you get into this kind of rhythm,
like you are the air, you are the forest, you're
going so quick you'd make a goshawk sick,
and suddenly you can see all the branches
and the little whippy twigs you can use, and
you seem to know your moves before you
can think of them, and you skid through the
trees like a bat! Like a lightning bat! Only
with more scrabbling! Suddenly you're on
that big old oak or pine or whatever you were
aiming for. YES! I hold the record! No one
ever got here quicker. Then maybe you tell
your friends and they have a go. And if you
can do that pretty well any day of the week
it's hard to be unhappy at all. Not really.
Even when you come to die you just close

your eyes, the old squirrels say, and go back to the Green Rush.'

Aubrey had been holding his breath while Hoppy babbled, and now he let it out.

'Phew!' he said. 'If only Dad was a squirrel. He hardly ever laughs.'

'When did he last climb a tree?' Hoppy asked.

'I can't remember.'

'It doesn't matter,' said the squirrel. 'We need to rev him up! And there's a simple way to do it. Three ways. Play, play and play!'

'It's easy saying that,' Aubrey told Hoppy. 'How are we going to do it?'

'Oh man, we're gonna glee him up! Make him wriggle like a labrador pup! Tackle his knees! Make him sneeze! Hide his keys, stuff his sock with peas. Put his shorts on your head, fill his bath with bread – the man who don't laugh is a man that's dead. Water trap him! Tie his shoelaces together...'

'But Hoppy, I don't think it's going to be

enough to beat the Terrible Yoot. Dad's
very tired. How are we going to make him
strong?'

'Positive thinking, Bree-Boy! If he thinks
he is getting stronger he will get stronger.
So just – make him!'

'But how?'

'Shave his toothbrush!' squeaked the
squirrel.

'Say that again.'

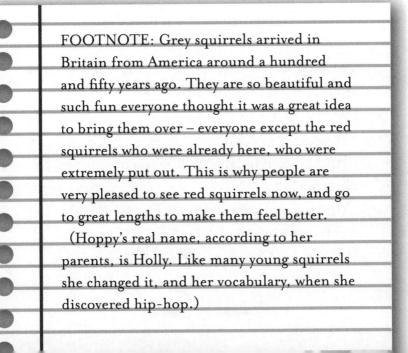

FOOTNOTE: Grey squirrels arrived in
Britain from America around a hundred
and fifty years ago. They are so beautiful and
such fun everyone thought it was a great idea
to bring them over – everyone except the red
squirrels who were already here, who were
extremely put out. This is why people are
very pleased to see red squirrels now, and go
to great lengths to make them feel better.

(Hoppy's real name, according to her
parents, is Holly. Like many young squirrels
she changed it, and her vocabulary, when she
discovered hip-hop.)

'Shave his toothbrush. Get an ox and shave his toothbrush handle.'

'Get a what?'

'An ox, man, a razor! Don't you listen to hip-hop? Sheesh! Whittle it so smooth he can't tell it's happened. Then when he picks it up it will feel light – and he'll think he's stronger!'

'Shave his toothbrush!' Aubrey laughed. 'I'm not allowed anything sharp. No oxes.'

'I'll get my crew,' said Hoppy. 'Just watch us chew! See these teeth? Got more edges than the Barrier Reef. We'll pull the padding out of his boots, they'll be lighter, and we'll hollow out the heels – much lighter! We'll take the lining out of his coat. I'll whittle his chip. We'll...'

'What chip?'

'His cell, Aubo! His "mobile telephone". With me?'

'Umm,' said Aubrey, 'I'm not sure. But if you think it will help...'

'Think it schmink it! I know it. Stay up,

baby. Climb some trees!' Hoppy bobbed at him, then with a dash she was off, chanting to herself, 'Chippa-chippa boom! Chippa-chippa BOOM-BOOM!'

That afternoon Jim was lying in his bed trying to sleep. He had been awake until six in the morning with Night Fears. Night Fears are worries, whirled together and concentrated into a soup of anxiety, pessimism and despair, a hopeless mixture of problems you cannot do anything about, and problems you can – if only you can get some sleep

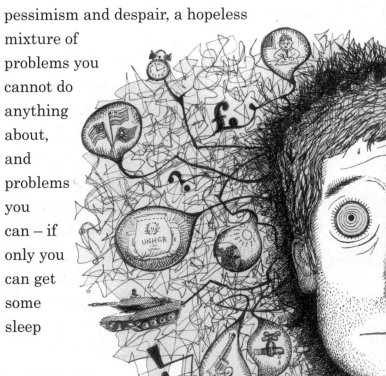

and deal with them when you are fresh.

Jim had floundered around in a soup of fears about global food supplies and climate change, road safety, Aubrey's education, Suzanne's pension, his own savings, the governments of China, America and Greece, organised crime, the news, diet, the roof, the world water supply, the oil price, refugee camps, car maintenance, fertiliser and pesticides, and that was only in the first hour. Jim's Night Fears kept him awake for six more.

So now he was trying to drop off. Though the afternoon was warm, blue and gold, in Jim's mind the world was a grey haze of exhaustion. His fears were so numerous they filled his mind like a vast and hideous army, stamping their feet, impatient for their turn to attack Jim's spirits. Jim lay with his eyes scrunched shut and his teeth clenched. Then he heard the fly.

A fly, this late in the year, he thought. And in the bedroom, just when I'm trying to sleep. Now it will probably land on me when I'm dropping off and wake me up. Maybe I should get up and let it out. Or kill it. No, I should let it out. Thou shalt not kill. Even flies. Oh Lord. I'm just...

Jim did not notice it, because he was too busy having this miserable conversation with himself, but this fly's behaviour was unusual. Instead of buzzing around randomly like flies do, led by curiosity and anything that smells interesting, this fly, whose name was Marcel, set up a regular circuit and stuck to it. His flight path was a tilted oval shape between the bed and the window. He flew down towards the bed – zzzzz – and then turned to fly up towards the window: bzzzz. The combined sound, zzzz-bzzzz, zzzz-bzzzz, made Jim fall fast asleep before he could complete the sentence, 'I'm just...'

Marcel landed on the windowsill and rubbed his legs together in satisfaction. Aubrey tiptoed in, holding his finger out.

On the end of it was a tiny blob of sugar and water paste. He deposited it carefully on the windowsill. Marcel began to feast. Aubrey tiptoed out.

Jim surfaced from his dreams three hours later. He had not slept so well for weeks! He had woken once, briefly, or perhaps he had dreamt it, because all he remembered was a hypnotic buzzing. There was no sign of the fly (Marcel was now having his own dreams, on top of the curtain rail, about cakes made of sour cream and rotten meat) and Jim had forgotten all about him. He felt properly refreshed. He decided he should join Suzanne and Aubrey and take responsibility for making tea for a change. He headed for the bathroom. He opened the bathroom door, jumped, stared in amazement and shouted a loud and incoherent sound like 'Squiibah!'

He appeared downstairs a few moments later.

'Squirrel!' he cried. 'In the bathroom!'

'Really, love?' Suzanne smiled, 'How funny!'

'Using my toothbrush!'

Suzanne started to laugh.

'It was! I went in and it put the toothbrush back – in the mug – and then it went out of the window like a rocket!'

'Trust you to be sharing your toothbrush with squirrels,' Suzanne said.

She thought it mildly surprising that a squirrel should have visited the bathroom. She assumed Jim was exaggerating about the replacement of the toothbrush. Had she seen the squirrel exiting the bathroom window, its cheeks packed with orange toothbrush shavings, which it then spat carefully into the drain – who knows what Suzanne would have thought? All we know is what Mr Ferraby thought. He happened to be in his garden and glancing towards his neighbours' house when the squirrel appeared.

'There is something going on with that squirrel of Aubrey's,' he told Mrs Ferraby. 'I just saw it come out of their bathroom and throw up carrots! Maybe they've got it on the wrong diet.'

Mrs Ferraby looked sceptical.

CHAPTER 8

Eighty Squirrels, One Heron

It was Mr Ferraby's habit, in the early evening, to go up to the top of his garden where he had his shed. One of his many interests was making mobiles out of card and string. His creations were beautiful and he had recently started selling them online to customers around the world. Early that evening, as Suzanne and Aubrey teased Jim about his squirrel, and Jim assembled ham and cheese omelettes, Mr Ferraby sat down in his shed and picked up his latest design. It was three elephants, made of coloured card. He almost had the balance right – balance is everything in mobiles – and was looking forward to sending it to a lady in Norway who wanted it for her new granddaughter. Mr Ferraby was smiling to himself when he just happened to glance out of the window of his shed towards Aubrey's house.

The smile stayed fixed on his face, in a foolish way, as Mr Ferraby forgot all about it.

He decided he must be going bonkers, right there, right then, in his shed, with his mobile in his hands. He must be as nutty as Bombay Mix and as loopy as a fruit hoop. He must be hallucinating, because what his eyes were telling his brain they could see could not possibly be happening.

Squirrels! So many! How many? Something like eighty squirrels were skittling through the gardens towards Aubrey's house. The ground teemed with a flooding tide of squirrels which broke against the walls and flowed up them in a snaky wave. A dozen squirrels vanished into the bathroom, where the first had come out. Two dozen more flung themselves into Aubrey's room through his window. Platoons

of squirrels plunged down the chimney.
Mr Ferraby's smile dropped off his face,
bounced on his workbench and rolled under
his chair.

Quick, he must save his neighbours from
massive squirrel attack! How do you fight
eighty squirrels? Mr Ferraby stared wildly
around his shed, picked up a trowel and

charged heroically towards violent death at the claws and teeth – small, but oh so sharp! – of multitudes of rabid squirrels.

He had almost made it to the battleground (he had to descend his own garden and climb over the low dividing wall, which took him a minute or two, because Mr Ferraby was not equipped with squirrel speed) when there was a huge scrabble of tiny feet and eighty squirrels hurled themselves out of Aubrey's house.

They fired out of the windows like bushy-tailed bullets. They shot out of the chimney like quick brown fireworks. They cascaded down the walls, leaping and scrabbling in their dozens. Some even used Mr Ferraby as a jumping-off point, landing on his head and shoulders and springing gaily away.

Mr Ferraby only heard squeaks and chitters but he had the strangest notion that some of these squirrels were grinning.

Now he steeled himself for the horrors he knew must await. He pictured Aubrey, Jim and Suzanne in a heap on the floor, torn to pieces, scattered around the kitchen and living room, their heads gnawed like nuts. He could not bear to imagine the scenes of blood and gore.

He pulled open the back door, trowel raised, prepared to duel with any killer squirrel which still feasted on the corpses of his neighbours.

'Hullo, Mr Ferraby!' Suzanne looked surprised, but pleased to see him, as she always was. 'Doing some gardening?'

'Squirrels?' Mr Ferraby managed, after a short pause.

'You too!' Jim cried. 'See, I told you! I had one in the bathroom earlier. Where was yours?'

'Oh! There were – one or two! Anyway. Sorry. Thought I saw something – er, so. All alright?' Mr Ferraby stammered.

He looked at Aubrey. Aubrey gave him a slightly shy smile.

'Fine, fine!' said Jim, who was visibly better than he had been for a while. 'It was using my toothbrush. Do squirrels get gum disease?'

'Not – as far as I know,' Mr Ferraby said, sounding a bit more like himself.

'Mr Ferraby, would you like to come in?' Suzanne asked. 'Would you like a cup of tea or a glass of something?'

Mr Ferraby thanked her, made his excuses and returned to his shed. He decided not to mention the episode to Mrs Ferraby. He was fairly sure he was not going mad. He did not believe he had been hallucinating – which meant he really had seen eighty squirrels invade his neighbours' house for two or three minutes, and then leave.

'But why?' he asked himself. 'Why, why, why?'

Marcel saw the answer in action the next morning. Suzanne had told Jim and Aubrey to look after each other and gone off to work. Aubrey declared he would be in the attic, doing his half-term maths project. Jim had an appointment with his doctor.

The fly watched Jim climb out of bed, have a bath and do his teeth. Marcel watched him dress, eat breakfast and put on his shoes and coat. Everything Jim did seemed charged with a new power. Marcel rubbed his legs together as he saw Jim's expression change repeatedly from puzzlement to satisfaction. Everything Jim did made him feel strong! His slippers, the book he read in the bath, his toothbrush, his shoes, coat, phone and wallet all felt light: at the touch of his hand the objects of the world seemed to spring to obey him.

'My strength is coming back!' Jim exclaimed. 'Could I really be getting better?'

FOOTNOTE: The combined gnawing power of eighty squirrels, multiplied by three minutes, is simply staggering. They could turn three wardrobes into one box of matches if the mood took them. Lightening Jim's life was no challenge at all.

Jim and Aubrey talked about how long Jim would be gone for, reminded themselves of what Aubrey was and was not allowed to do when home alone (no fires, bombs or electrical stunts – common sense!) and Jim set off down the lane with half a spring in his step. He even managed to take in some of the still beauty of the quiet autumn day.

Jim had not been gone long when the surprising events at Woodside Terrace began again. From his vantage point in the shed, Mr Ferraby made the following observations.

10.08 Jim leaves

10.17 Aubrey in garden

10.32 Heron lands in garden! Aubrey approaches. It does not fly off. Are they talking???

10.38 Heron flies off.
Aubrey goes inside

11.04 Aubrey in garden – heron – fish! What a terrible thing it is to lose one's reason, to be the victim of visions too strange to credit, hallucinations too extraordinary to relate! I must tell.

Wow. 12.30 Jim back. And now look at them – Aubrey hammer – Jim pond – of course! Lunch.

If you have had the luck to become acquainted with a Grey Heron you will know what wry, dry birds they are, for all that they spend so much time with their feet in the water. And of course they are very big and angular and their beaks are as sharp as Roman shortswords.

The heron's landing in the garden, the swoop and swish of it, the bounce, brake-flap and the great bird suddenly towering over him would have made Aubrey jump a few days ago – but what a few days they had been.

'Hullo!' Aubrey cried, grinning up at the heron's ring-gold eye, 'Welcome to Woodside Terrace!'

'Call me Ardea,' said the heron, in a rather laconic way. 'Good of you to invite me.'

'Oh I didn't, it's all Athene Noctua...'

'I know,' said the heron. You could see he was amused. 'Why would anyone invite a lanky-shanky bignose into their garden on their own initiative?'

'But I didn't mean that at all!' Aubrey cried.

'I know,' said the heron, trying hard not to show his enjoyment. 'Sarcasm – lowest form of wit before you come to slapstick, which I happen to rather like. Do you know the difference between a banana and a missing manhole cover?'

'Uuum...'

'Then I'm not coming to yours for pudding. I hear you are in want of a fish?'

It was Aubrey's turn to stop himself laughing.

'Yes,' he said, seriously. 'Dad needs to eat fresh fish. They don't sell any in town. It's all frozen.'

'Type of fish?' squawked the heron. 'Species of fish? Size of fish? Gender of fish? You do know there is more to fish than Fresh, Frozen and Shell, right?'

'Sarcasm,' Aubrey retorted, 'highest form of humour for low-witted wading birds.'

'Hey I like that,' the heron said, sounding impressed. 'You wouldn't write that down for me, and sign it?'

Aubrey ignored this. 'We need oily fish.'

'Oily it will be,' said the heron. 'Try not to get too bored without me. I will be twenty-six minutes precisely. Clear the runway – CLEAR!'

The bird sprang into the air, wings beating tremendously, lifted over the terrace roofs and climbed away, long legs sticking out behind him.

Twenty-six minutes later, to Mr Ferraby's

astonishment and Aubrey's admiration,
Ardea the heron landed in the garden again.

'How could you be so precise?' Aubrey
wanted to know.

The heron had his head tipped back. He
said, 'Gaark!'

'Gaark?' Aubrey repeated. 'Have you run
out of words?'

'GANK!' coughed the heron, and its
eye flamed a ferocious gold.

'I don't think I've come across that one
either! Could you write it down for me, and
sign it?'

The heron narrowed its eye, took four

quick steps, threw its long neck out over the pond, opened its beak and heaved up a stunning silver-green fish, over a foot long and vigorously alive. This fish fell into the pond with a splosh and immediately began swimming around in fast circles. The pond was barely bigger than a birdbath. The fish looked like a whale shark in there.

'Fish times one,' said the heron, with dignity. 'Trout, rainbow, male. Oily. Delicious however you cook it, even better raw. Liberated from the Beck Fishfarm, twelve minutes flying time from here in these conditions. Does that conclude our business?'

'Sorry, Ardea. Ha ha! Gank! You've got to admit it was quite funny!'

'Fair point.' The heron nodded. 'It was. So, are you going to be OK with killing this fish, or would you prefer to look away while I do it?'

'Oh. I don't know. You just –

whack it on the head, do you?'

'That works,' the heron agreed. 'Get a good grip – which is as hard as it looks – and bash it on a rock. And don't let it talk you out of eating it. We all have to live. Stuff eats stuff. Way of the world. Don't let any fish-wailing soften your heart.'

'Fish-wailing?'

'Yes, the usual. "My poor fishkids, they need me, have mercy. My fish-wife, how will she survive? Oh! Oh! To think I'll never see her again, please don't kill me, I beg you." That kind of thing. On and on. Don't listen. Take him by the tail and whack.'

'I don't know if I can do it now. Poor fish!'

'Hmm, well, don't blame you. Can't stand it myself. It's one of the reasons we like to swallow them as quickly as possible. Spear, swallow, that's it for me. And for them! Why don't you let your father do it? He won't hear a thing.'

'I suppose he might do it...'

'Your mother's a straight-shooting sort of

bird isn't she? She'd do it, wouldn't she?'

'Right,' said Aubrey, making a sudden decision. 'I'll do it. It's OK to kill things if you're going to eat them. Isn't it?'

'I don't know about OK,' said the heron, 'Vegetarians would disagree. But a top predator like me doesn't get that menu. I find killing fish rather beats starving to death. Different for you of course. You have to make a moral choice.'

Ardea left. Jim returned. Aubrey showed him the new occupant of the pond.

'Oh Aubrey! Where did you get that?' Jim demanded, dizzily.

'A heron dropped it,' Aubrey said. 'It's a rainbow trout!'

'It is – and so beautiful!'

'Yes,' Aubrey agreed, with a pang of conscience, 'But won't it taste delicious?'

'Mmm,' said Jim, 'It would. With some new potatoes and lightly fried courgettes it would be scrumptious!'

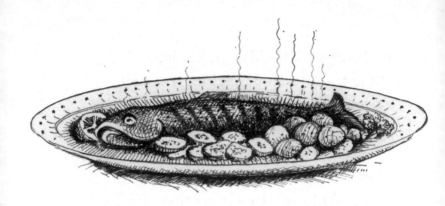

'Shall we catch it, Dad?'

'Well, yes, I guess.' Jim looked worried now. 'I'll have to kill it, you realise? I'll try to make sure it doesn't suffer, but I think you'd better not watch.'

'Sure,' Aubrey said, humbly grateful. 'I'll get you the hammer.'

And off he zipped, followed by a surprised look from his father, who was not to know that Aubrey had thought this fish death through.

Aubrey returned with the tool. It was a lumpen, heavy and serious hammer. You could put an elephant down with it if you tapped him in the right place.

Jim had been staring at the trout. Now he

turned to his son and swallowed.

Oh dear, Aubrey thought.

'I can't do it,' Jim said. 'It's too beautiful. We should put it in a bucket of water and take it down to the beck.'

'But Dad, don't you need to eat oily fish?'

'I – I think I am supposed to, yes. But I don't want to kill it! The poor thing.'

'But you eat meat. And fish!'

'I do – but – it's different when it – when you...'

'No problem,' Aubrey said, briskly. 'I've got this.'

Before he had time to change his mind, before Jim had time to say anything, and, crucially, before the fish had time to protest, Aubrey lunged forward, grabbed the trout, hoiked it out and dealt it a solid whack with the hammer. The trout did not even have time to think anything – at least, not out loud. Aubrey thought he might have heard it say, 'Oy!' but that was that. He gave it another whack to be sure, and looked up at his father.

Jim seemed impressed.

'Well,' he said, 'let's call your mum and tell her to pick up some courgettes. We're really going to eat!'

CHAPTER 9

Exercise is Good For You

Supper that night was excellent. Afterwards, Jim felt brave enough to take a cup of coffee into the garden. He stood admiring the autumn stars, and the planets in their gold and twinkling red. Mr Ferraby happened to be putting out his compost. He bid Jim good evening without mentioning the heron, the fish, the conversations Jim's son had seemed to have with the bird, or the surprising way in which the child had dispatched the trout.

'Lovely evening, Mr Ferraby,' Jim remarked.

'Oh yes,' Mr Ferraby said. 'Lovely day.'

'It was,' Jim said, and thought to himself It actually was! Perhaps I'm getting better... But then another voice inside him, a voice which was also his, but which was controlled by the Terrible Yoot, began to hiss insidiously in a corner of his mind...

'Silly weak man, skulking at home, letting your little child use extreme violence against innocent fish - and why weren't you at work earning your living and providing for your family?'

'Well,' said Mr Ferraby, 'Goodnight then.'

'Good night! Mr Ferraby – ah – goodnight...' Jim trailed off.

'Are you planning to rely on herons delivering fish to feed your wife and child while you hide in bed and whimper?' Jim's Yoot-prompted, cruel and spiteful thoughts continued.

'AH!' Jim cried. He downed the rest of his coffee and stumbled inside.

Mr Ferraby watched him go.

'Jim seems troubled,' he told Mrs Ferraby later. 'I hope Aubrey's not wearing him down with all this animal magic.'

Mr Ferraby had not mentioned the heron and fish business to his wife. She gave him a thoughtful look.

'Jim!' Suzanne exclaimed, the next morning, 'A heron just dropped a huge fish in the garden!'

Sure enough, there was another trout in the pond. This time Jim did the necessary piscicide and brought the trout in. They had it for supper that night.

The same thing happened the next day, too. Aubrey had to have a word with Ardea.

'We aren't herons! We can't eat fish every day.'

'You would if you were smart,' the heron said, loftily. 'Or if you wanted to be smart – you'd all become piscivores right now. But of course you're only humans.'

'It's very kind of you, Ardea. But isn't it a risk? Who owns the fish farm? Aren't they going to get cross?'

'They had a go at me with a shotgun the other day,' Ardea said, mildly. 'Something must have upset them – I can't imagine what. As a Grey Heron I am protected at all times by the Wildlife and Countryside Act 1981, making it illegal to kill, catch or hold me in captivity. Perhaps they meant to miss, to scare me off.'

'Please be careful! And – well – I think we can manage on three fish a week for now.'

'Would you like me to clean the house while I'm here? Take out the rubbish? Do the shopping? Fetch the paper? Pick crumbs out of the car?'

'The fish will be fine, Ardea! Thank you!'

'We fly to serve,' Ardea said, like an actor pretending to be tired. Then he bellowed: 'Now clear the runway – CLEAR!' and took off with a jump, a huge flapping, and a cackle.

Jim decided that having heron-delivered fresh trout three times a week was so strange that the best thing he could do was accept it, and not make too much fuss. Suzanne mentioned the first two incidents to her friends at work, but then she left it. Aubrey never even thought of telling his friend Harrison: Harrison was not really into herons. Mr Ferraby thought about telling the newspapers, or starting a Remarkable Heron blog, but he did not. Something was going on next door and he wanted to know what would happen next, so he kept quiet, and kept watch.

The business with the raven began when Jim was taking his daily walk. Jim knew he needed regular exercise but he panicked a bit at being seen out in the world, wandering around, when all his friends and colleagues were hard at work. Aubrey overheard him telling Suzanne he was ashamed of being 'signed off sick'.

'I should hide in the house until I'm better,' he said, guiltily.

Suzanne said hiding in the house was no way to get better.

So Jim took little walks up and down the lane. They barely counted as exercise,

Suzanne and Aubrey thought, but they seemed to make him happy, and he paused every few metres to study plants and birds and the sights of the valley – which was an improvement on staring at his feet. He took his precious binoculars with him and birdwatched. These binoculars were incredibly light and wonderfully powerful. Jim said they gave him the eyes of a falcon.

As he wandered down the lane with his binoculars, falcon-eyeing the woods, the skyline and the birds moving through the trees along the stream, Jim failed to spot that he was being followed. He would have made a lousy falcon.

He was leaning on a low stone wall, staring at the meadow below, his binoculars dangling idly from one hand, when his stalker struck. There was a sudden jerk – a mighty tug at his left hand – and his binoculars were gone: snatched!

'Hey!' he cried, spinning round.

Jim's binoculars were hanging in mid-air.

'Hey!'

His binoculars, his precious binoculars, were dangling from their strap. The strap was held tight in the claws of a huge black bird, bigger than any crow, with a hackle of feathers like a beard at its throat, a beak like a fat curved dagger and a look of dark amusement in its eye – a raven!

The raven flew off down the road, gathering up the binocular strap and looping it over its neck. Now the bird landed on a wall forty yards away.

'Give them back!' shouted Jim.

'PRRUUK!' shouted the raven.

Jim ran at it.

The raven waited until Jim was almost within reach, flapped off, landed forty more yards away, bobbed his head and shouted 'PRRUUK!' again.

Jim covered these yards even faster.

'HAARR!' called the raven, as Jim closed with it, and set off again. By stopping and starting, by landing and taking off again, by swooping and teasing, the raven made Jim run nearly a mile, right down to the edge of town, before flying over his head and making him run nearly a mile back the other way. Not for a moment did Jim consider giving up.

Laying the binoculars gently on Jim's doorstep the raven looked him in the eye, croaked something that sounded like 'Thaar yaa aaar!' and flew away. Jim put his hands on his knees, bent double and panted like a hot dog. He was shattered. The muscles in his legs felt as though someone had set fire to them. His lungs burned, his vision wavered and he thought he might be sick. But he had surely taken some vigorous exercise – and exercise, as everyone knows, is very good for you.

'Corax,' the raven said, 'Corax Corax.'

'Your parents named you twice?' Aubrey asked. He was not exactly scared of the bird but he was wary of it. Anyone would be. It was huge, with a loud throaty voice and an accent that sounded as if it came from somewhere near the Tower of London. They were in the attic, the raven gripping the edge of the skylight, its fearsome claws digging into the wooden frame. With its great sharp bill and spiky beard Aubrey thought it was like talking to a pirate king.

'We're all Corax. My brother is Corax Corax Corax. My sister is Corax Corax Corax Corax. My nephew is...'

'I see,' said Aubrey. 'So, er, what are you into?'

'Death and acrobatics!' crowed Corax. 'You know the secret of 'appiness? Death! The Grim Reaper, the Lady in Brown, the Final Trumpet, the End! Good old graveyards – cheer anyone up! Anywhere you can guarantee a lot of death, that's the place to go. Dead people, dead animals, squashed hedgehogs, bloated bodies, rotten sheep, splattered things – find some of them. Have a good gawp. Now, don't you feel better?

That's not you is it? Under a gravestone, whitening down to a set of bones? That's not you with the tyre track tattoo, squished flat, eyes popped and a belly full of maggots! No. You're alive. And dead things are your friends. They fertilise the soil and fill the stomach. You eat dead plants, dead animals. Maybe you don't pick 'em up when they're rotting, but it's the same thing – I just like the stronger flavours. What do you like?'

'I like chocolate,' Aubrey said.

'Dead cocoa beans!' Corax croaked. 'Lovely! 'Course it's harder being a raven now than it used to be. They don't 'ang people like they did in my great-great-great grandfather's time. They used to leave 'em swinging on the gallows to get pecked.

People went to look at the bodies, even
while Grandad was eating 'em, because
it cheered them up – they felt alive! And
gibbets, where gamekeepers used to 'ang
the animals they shot, they've gone. There's
so much clearing up these days you 'ardly
get more than a couple of pecks at a roadkill
before someone pinches it. Tell your dad to
go and get an eyeful of death, and a good
strong sniff of it. Tell 'im from your uncle
Corax – in a century or so the grubs that ate
him will have been eaten by moles which
will have died of old age and been eaten by
grubs and all that's left of 'im will be grub
poo, and that's all that'll be left of most of
us, grub poo! That's the future, tell 'im. He
will feel fantastic. We're only here for a few
decades if we're lucky. Makes it a lot easier
to enjoy life when you think of it like that –
makes you want to do some acrobatics! Pity
you can't fly, I could teach you to loop the
loop.'

'I'd like that,' said Aubrey.

'By the time I've finished exercising 'im, your father will be turning somersaults!'

'That's good,' Aubrey said, 'But I'm not sure about all this death stuff.'

'No one is!' cackled Corax, 'You might not be sure of death, but you can be sure Death's sure of you! Ca-ha-ha!'

'I can see it works for you, Corax,' said Aubrey. 'But it might make some people feel a bit gloomy.'

'That's because I am a joyful pessimist, which is someone who sees the gloomy side of things and laughs. 'Ave you met Mr Velvet 'Umps?'

'Mr Velvet Humps? Who is he?'

'Mr Velvet 'Umps is a mole. What you might call a Measured Optimist.'

'What does that mean?'

'Someone who sees the bright side of things but likes to keep it calm. He lives in the field. Why don't you go and 'ave a word? See what he thinks your old man should do.'

Corax flew away. Aubrey went to the end

of the garden, climbed over the fence and
made his way along the edge of the wood to
the field. He sat down next to a molehill and
waited. Soon the earth crumbled and shifted
and a small snout poked out, with whiskers
on the end, followed by a sleek black nose
and two tiny eyes, blinking.

'Mr Humps?'

'Aubrey Rambunctious Wolf?' The mole's
voice was soft. He spoke gently. 'Did you
want a word?'

'I was talking to Corax Corax about gloom
and death,' Aubrey explained. 'He said I
should speak to you. It's about my father.'

'Yes, I heard about poor Jim. When
I'm feeling a bit low,' said the mole,
thoughtfully, 'I dig. Get down under some
thick warm clods, then get down deeper.
Did you know it gets warmer the deeper you
go? Not many problems in this life can't be
solved by a bit of digging. Dig down until it
gets warm and sleep there. Sleep as much
as possible. If you stay down long enough,

when you come back up, things look a bit
different. You know, old world turns a bit,
light looks different, trees look different,
the season's moved, the air smells good. And
you're hungry. So you eat a worm, and you
think by heck that's a good worm. This is a
good morning. Maybe you eat another, and
you think, it might even turn out to be a
good day. And when you've got one of them
behind you, there's twice the chance the one
in front will be good, too.'

Aubrey thought this sounded very sensible advice. He talked with Velvet Humps for a while, watching the last of the sun making long shadows out of the molehills.

CHAPTER 10
The Attack

Autumn darkened towards winter and tall rains fell hard and long. The trees of Rushing Wood were stark sentinels now, like cold old men with nowhere to go. They groaned in the wind. Sleet and hail swept in across the moors. The mornings were dim and noons were dull. The nights fell hungrily on the days. Despite the efforts of the squirrels to make Jim feel strong, and the raven's campaign to make him fit (Jim had been forced to chase his hat, his scarf, his bag, his keys and his wallet, which Corax Corax pinched from his pocket) and despite his fish-rich diet, the coming of winter drove Jim down to a desperate place.

Suzanne and Aubrey could see that he was sinking. He never laughed. He could barely eat half his trout. The doctors gave him pills to take but they only seemed to make him numb. They gave him pills to help him sleep, and pills to wake him up, and pills which were supposed to make him happier. Nothing helped.

Aubrey knew that the Yoot had Jim in its grip, but Aubrey did not know how badly his father was suffering. Every day now, from the moment he woke up, Jim had to listen to the Yoot.

'You have failed, Jim,' it whispered to him. 'Your life is a wreck. You are making Aubrey and Suzanne very unhappy. Why don't you leave them to get on with their lives without being weighed down by a sad, selfish sack like you? Have you thought of going away?' the Yoot hissed.

The most cunning and deadly part of the Yoot's attack on Jim was that Jim did not know where it came from. He had no concept of the Yoot: he thought the Yoot's voice was just his thoughts, in his head. Because the rest of his mind was in such a turmoil of misery the Yoot's voice was becoming the only thing he could hear clearly.

'Have you thought of getting out of this mess you're making?' said the Yoot, disguised as Jim's thoughts. 'There is a way out, you know - yes, yes, you do! There are so many ways out, after all...'

Now the Yoot's voice in Jim's head became soft. Its words were as sticky and sweet as golden syrup.

'Why don't you come for a little walk on the moors? We could find a sheltered spot. I'll show you one, the perfect place to curl up. You can just fall asleep. I'll keep you warm. I will hold you tight as you drop off, and you won't have to suffer any more. Wouldn't that be better than this?

'Imagine - peace at last! A lovely deep sleep - aren't you dying for that, Jim? Oh how you are! And then perhaps Suzanne will meet a good strong man, the kind who laughs a lot. She will meet a man Aubrey will admire, someone who will bring him up to be happy, with lots of opportunities. Someone successful, a champion - that's what your little boy needs, not a slug like you! Think of Aubrey! Doesn't he deserve the greatest man in the world? And that's not you, is it Jim? Aren't you being rather selfish, lying about like a corpse refusing to rot? Aren't you sick of making everyone miserable? Stop being so selfish. Come, Jim, come away with me to the moors...'

Every day Jim fought that voice. He tried not to listen to it. He tried not to believe it, but the Yoot's whispers never stopped. On the first night of the school Christmas holidays, when everyone else in the country seemed so excited and joyful, and carols played everywhere and the town was strung with twinkling lights, Jim realised he could take no more.

The Yoot had asked him what sort of Christmas he could offer Aubrey – did his wonderful son really deserve such a tortured man hanging around him, ruining

Christmas, killing everyone's happiness?

'The sooner you get it over with, the sooner Suzanne and Aubrey will be able to start their new life!' the Yoot told him. 'Come away, Jim, this has gone on too long now. It is time for you to be brave. You must do the right thing for your family.'

'Alright,' Jim said, at last. 'Alright. They will be better off when I am gone. I know they will be terribly sad at first but at least it will all be over. And Suzanne and Aubrey are all that matters. It is true – it is time I got out of their way.'

In the early evening Jim pulled on his coat.

'I'm just going for a walk,' he said to Suzanne. She and Aubrey were making Christmas decorations.

'Oh!' Suzanne said, surprised.

It was not much of an evening for a walk; the clouds were low and heavy with snow and there was an eerie yellow light in the sky. 'Wouldn't you like to stay and give us a hand instead? Look what Aubrey's making!'

Aubrey was covered in glue and glitter, coloured tissue paper and tinsel.

'I AM THE HUMAN CHRISTMAS TREE!' he boomed at his father. 'LAY YOUR PRESENTS AT MY FEET OR I WILL CLIMB DOWN YOUR CHIMNEY!'

Jim laughed, weakly.

'See? They are so happy, just the two of them,' the Yoot whispered in Jim's ear. 'The only sad thing here is you... Help them, Jim! Leave them to their happiness. Take your misery away!'

'Very good, Aubrey,' Jim said, 'You are the best human Christmas tree in the world.' He hugged Aubrey hard and kissed him. 'Well done, darling,' he said to Suzanne. 'You're wonderful. You're so kind and – just – you're the most ... I love you. I love you both so much.' Now he kissed Suzanne and hugged her too. 'Just going for a little walk,' he said. 'Things will get better. I know they will. Don't wait up for me. I need a good long walk. I love you...' he said, and before they could say anything else, with his heart breaking in his chest, and his sobs held back, but only just, Jim hurried out of the house.

Jim rushed down the lane. He was crying, the tears running hot down his cheeks.

'Well done, Jim!' the Yoot whispered to him. 'You've done the hard part! The rest is easy. And remember - this is all for them - you're doing it for your wife and your son.'

Now the Yoot began telling him where to go.

'Take the path which goes along the edge of the wood, and follow it straight up to the moors.'

Jim strode along as fast as he could go. His nose ran and tears filled his eyes. He was sobbing so much he weaved from side to side, but the Yoot kept driving him on.

Aubrey and Suzanne carried on making decorations but they were both a bit quiet now.

'Dad doesn't look too good,' Aubrey said, after a while.

'No,' said Suzanne. 'Poor man. But he's trying so hard. I am very proud of him.'

'Me too! And he's supposed to take

exercise...' said Aubrey.

'Yes,' Suzanne agreed. She was frowning, but she made an effort and smiled brightly. 'Yes, exactly! And he'll sleep well when he's had a good walk. Now, who wants some hot crumpets, dripping with butter and honey?'

'Yay! Crumpets!' Aubrey sang out, and the two of them smiled at each other.

Suzanne went into the kitchen and put the crumpets in the toaster.

Aubrey ran upstairs to his room and stared out of the window at the wood. His heart was beating fast, there was a pulse in his chest and a hot feeling in his stomach. Something was wrong.

Suzanne took the crumpets out of their packet. She fitted four of them into the toaster and pushed the rack down. She stared out of the kitchen window. The night was closing in. There were no birds in the garden. Everything was still but the wind.

Something's wrong, something's wrong, something's wrong, ran Aubrey's thoughts like a chant. Something's wrong...

And suddenly he knew what it was.

The Yoot is here, he thought, wildly, I can feel it – the Yoot has come. It's out there in the wood or on the moor: it's close. *The Yoot has come for my dad.*

Downstairs the crumpets popped out of the toaster but Suzanne did not even notice. She was filled with a sense of terrible worry as she stared at the gathering dark. She suddenly wished, desperately, that Jim had not gone out.

'Aubrey!' she shouted.

'Mum!' Aubrey yelled, and he was charging down the stairs, jumping them three at a time. He burst into the kitchen. 'Dad's in trouble! We've got to find him! We've got to get him back!'

You will remember that when she needed to move fast Suzanne could pretty well jump over houses. Before he had drawn three breaths, it seemed, Aubrey was no longer a human Christmas tree: he was being bundled out of the front door, wearing his coat, shoes and hat. He had an impression of his mother zipping around the room; she seemed to have three pairs of hands, two of them dressing him, two dressing her, and two grabbing her keys, a torch and her telephone. In less time than it will take you to read this sentence, Suzanne had noticed a bottle was gone, which prompted her to fly up to the bathroom, see that Jim's pills were gone too, dive back down the stairs, pour a lot of salt into a plastic bottle, fill it with water and sweep Aubrey out of the house.

'We have to hurry,' she told him. 'I'm going to carry you, OK?'

Suzanne lifted him up into a piggyback; now they were hurtling down the road.

Aubrey knew his mother had been a marathon runner before he was born. She could sprint, too: she always won the

Mothers' Race on Sports Day at school, crossing the finishing line with a wave and a smile, not even panting. But he had never seen her in action like this. Below him her feet were pounding, faster and faster. In seconds they reached the end of the road where three paths divided. One went into the trees. One went down to the stream. The last path ran along the edge of the wood up toward the moors. In the car park, where the paths began, Aubrey could just make out a magnificent pheasant in the gloom. It shouted 'KOK-KOK!'

Suzanne paused. 'Which way do you think he went?'

Aubrey did not hesitate. Ever since he had told Athene Noctua that he would fight the Yoot he had had a sense of it, out there somewhere. Now he could feel it like the heat of a fire, close.

'Up!' he cried. 'Take that path! Along the edge of the wood!'

'KOK-KOK!' crowed the pheasant, bobbing at them.

In his mind, Aubrey heard it say, in a clucky rush, 'About fifteen minutes ago, one man, one Yoot, going for the moors – be quick!'

They were off again. Suzanne swerved up the third path. Her feet leapt from rock to rock. As the path became steeper she seemed to go faster. Soon the wood was thinning and fields rolled by on either side. Now they were into the upper part of the wood, the trees and bushes swirling around them in a dark blur. Night was coming down, the darkness gathering huge and fast.

Suzanne was breathing hard but she did not slow down. Her torch clicked, the light dancing wildly in front of them as she ran on and on, and up and up, as the path became steeper and steeper and the trees

hunched low. It was a wild ride for Aubrey.
Bouncing around on his mother's back was
like riding a flying horse. Suzanne's arms
clamped the backs of his knees and she held
him tight.

At the top of the wood the path flattened.
Ridges and shoulders of land folded away
into nothingness. They had reached the
moor.

The moor is wild country, haunted with
winds which have lived here since the
beginning of time. In all those centuries,
Aubrey felt, no one had ever come up here
on a night as grim as this.

Suzanne stopped. She was panting.

'Where now, do you think?'

Aubrey closed his eyes. He shut out the cold and he shut out the moans of the wind. He felt as though the monster was all around him now, like a beast circling, just out of sight. Its presence was strongest ... to the left, he was sure of it, ahead and to the left.

'Somewhere left, sort of diagonally,' he said.

'Six hundred metres, to be precise, diagonally left,' said a gentle, female voice in his head.

'Who are you?' Aubrey thought back.

'My name is Lepus,' said the voice. 'I'm a hare. Excuse me for not showing myself. I am rather shy. Your father is in a dip in the ground that way – go fast! Go like a hare!'

'Six hundred metres diagonally left!'

Aubrey cried, 'Quick Mum, go!'

Suzanne had no idea how Aubrey could be so certain but she believed him completely. The moor was covered in heather stalks and tight-bunched whinberry bushes, so she could not sprint. But she went as fast as she could without falling, picking her way by the light of the torch, stumbling, slipping, striding and leaping across the great wastes of the moor. Her torch was a tiny glint in the vastness of the dark.

CHAPTER 11
A Battle of Life and Death

They found Jim exactly where Lepus had said they would. He was lying curled up next to a rock at the bottom of a gully. Aubrey shouted, desperately, 'Dad!'

Suzanne's torch lit up Jim's huddled shape, with his knees drawn up to his chest.

He was wrapped in his coat, his chin tucked down on his chest. He lay utterly still. The bottle was in his hand, half empty. The pill bottle was there too. Pills lay scattered on the ground.

Suzanne put Aubrey down and thrust the torch into his hand. She bent over her husband.

'Jim!' she shouted. 'JIM!'

She put her finger to his neck, just below his ear, searching for his pulse.

'He's alive,' she panted.

'Dad!' Aubrey shouted. 'Wake up!'

Suzanne spoke calmly and clearly. 'Now Aubrey this is not going to be pleasant but I have to wake him up and make him sick – we need to get those pills out of him. Stand there and shine the torch on him. You'd better not look – close your eyes.'

But Aubrey could not do that. He stared as Suzanne shook Jim hard by the shoulders. She shouted, 'Jim! JIM! WAKE UP! Open your eyes – OPEN YOUR EYES! Look at me! JIM! OPEN YOUR EYES AND LOOK AT ME!'

As she shouted Suzanne slapped Jim's face – once, twice, three times.

'Come on, sweetheart,' she cried, 'Aubrey and I are here! We've come to wake you up! WAKE UP!'

At first Jim made only the slightest sound, a little grumble. But as she slapped him and shouted his name he groaned more loudly, and now his eyes blinked open. In the light of the torch he stared up vacantly. He looked like a very young baby, as if he could not really see.

'Yes, yes, good man! Very good! Look at me, darling – that's right. Come back to us now, come back – say something Jim – say my name.'

'Shuzzz...' Jim mumbled. 'Shuzzam, Aubee...'

'That's it darling! You're coming back, you're waking up, aren't you?'

'Feelshick,' Jim mumbled, 'shleepingills.'

'I know love, I know. Now, let's sit you up...'

Suzanne hauled him up until he was sitting. He slumped forward as if his head was very heavy.

'Right, now, this is going to be horrible and it is going to save your life. I want you to drink this, and I want you to swallow it.'

Suzanne held the bottle of salty water to Jim's lips and began to pour it in. Jim shook his head and the water spilled, but Suzanne clamped an arm around his neck, tilted his head back and shouted, in a voice so stern and commanding that Aubrey jumped, she yelled, 'SWALLOW ALL OF IT NOW!'

Jim's eyes widened at her tone and the taste, and he looked dazed, but he began to swallow and swallow obediently ... two, three, four glugs he managed, and then an appalled looked crossed his face.

He wrenched himself free of Suzanne's grip, rolled onto all fours, and he began to be stunningly sick.

Jim heaved, Jim spluttered, Jim retched and Jim hurled. He spewed, he puked and he threw up. Jim barfed, Jim chundered and Jim blew chunks. As soon as she saw her patient was responding to treatment, Suzanne switched to Aubrey; she knelt beside him, gently took the torch from his hand, put her arm round his shoulders and turned him away from his father.

She hugged him tight.

'We did it, darling!' she said. 'We found him in time – you found him in time, you extraordinary boy. You've saved him, you know – he could have been anywhere – I would never, ever have found him without you. How on earth did you know he was here?'

Behind them Jim was still vomiting, but less violently now, and in between being sick he was making other noises – not weak mumbles, but sounds like 'Yuk!' and 'Eiuw! Disgusting ... oh goodness ... errk!'

His voice was clear and he was very much awake.

Aubrey did not answer his mother at first. Tides of feelings surged through him. He had never been so relieved. Part of him felt dizzy with thankfulness. And he was shocked at everything that had happened, from the dreadful moment in his room when he realised the Yoot was attacking, to the wild race through the wood on his mother's back, to the terror of seeing Jim huddled up in the dip, and the violence of Suzanne's life-saving treatment, and the sight of his father being sick. And below it all, Aubrey felt in the centre of his being an anger like nothing he had ever known.

Aubrey's anger was like the bright flame in his heart. The Yoot had tried to kill his father. It had taken Jim to the edge of life and nearly, so nearly tempted him to his death. The battle was well and truly joined now.

'You've had your shot, Yoot,' Aubrey thought. 'Now it's my turn. The time has come. We'll have it out tonight. I'll meet you wherever you want, but I will meet you, and then we'll see what you're made of...'

He took a deep breath.

'He's going to be OK is he, Mum?'

Jim spoke from behind them.

'I'm going to be just fine, Aubrey Boy.'

They turned around. Jim was standing up. He was using the rest of the salty water to clean his hands and face.

'I don't know what came over me,' he said, slowly. 'But I know I will never, ever, do anything like that again. You've saved my life. Both of you. I am so sorry I frightened you. I will never be able to apologise enough, or thank you enough … I haven't got the words. When I heard your voices I knew I wanted to come back – I wanted to live. I will always want to live, thanks to you two. I know I haven't been well, but I know I am the luckiest man in the world tonight. Aubrey, Suzanne, darling, you … you bring me back to the light.'

Aubrey and Suzanne looked at him. They

were full of so many feelings they did not know what to say.

'Group hug!' shouted Suzanne, and they rushed together and clung tight, the three of them, there in the dark dip in the moor.

'Now,' said Jim, 'does anyone have any idea how we get back to Woodside Terrace?'

Suzanne laughed. 'Aubrey does!' she said. 'He seems to know all sorts of extraordinary things.'

Aubrey took their hands, one on each side, and led them all the way home.

CHAPTER 12

Face to Face with the
TERRIBLE YOOT

After lots of Suzanne's homemade soup, which was more like a steaming sweet stew, and hot baths, the family went to bed. For the first time in ages Aubrey heard his parents laughing in their room.

Suzanne had been calling Jim a ninny, a nit and a nincompoop, and Jim had been hugging her, and picking Aubrey up and whirling him round and chattering about what a hero he was, and what a superwoman his mother was: being so near death had given him a real shock of life.

Aubrey had not been ready to join in with his father's high spirits, but he smiled to hear them both as he lay in bed. His mother and father were safe. But now his smile faded, and his anger leapt up like a blaze. It was time to meet this thing, whatever it was.

From the moment they had found Jim, the Yoot's presence had seemed to vanish. You would have thought it had never existed. But the boy was not going to let it get away as easily as that. As his tired body slipped towards sleep Aubrey's mind spoke out to his enemy.

'I know you can hear me, you disgusting bully,' he thought. 'You are lurking somewhere, plotting your next attack. I am Aubrey Rambunctious Wolf and I call you to fight me tonight! Answer me, answer me if you dare! I'll fight you here, I'll fight you there, I'll fight you in your horrid lair!'

There was a pause, like a listening silence. Aubrey held his breath. Now a faint sound came – a laugh, a low laugh, coming closer.

'You call the meeting,' said a syrupy voice, which seemed amused, 'but I decide where we have it.'

'Go on then!'

'I choose ... the Desert of Misfortune,'
came the voice, as if it were gloating.

Immediately Aubrey was floating up into
dreamscape. Far below he saw his house and
Woodside Terrace and Rushing Wood, but
he could see the wood's shapes changing as
he watched, the trees becoming taller and
darker, and growing mighty now, becoming
great pines and firs with mountains behind
them, their peaks all glittering with snow
and starlight.

'The Enchanted Mountains!' Aubrey
exclaimed. They were so beautiful that he
longed to swoop down and land there, but
now they were falling away, smaller and
smaller they shrank to white rumples, and
faster and faster he flew over dark plains
down to a lacquer sea, a sheeny, oily sea
which rushed below him at a thousand
miles a moment, until the darkness ahead
lightened as if dawn were galloping towards

him, the light leaping over a shoreline of rocks with the sun behind them, and now sea and shore were far away behind him and he was crossing sand, ridges and valleys of sand: everywhere he looked was sand, scrub and desert. The sun had climbed faster than a bouncing ball, right up to the top of the sky, and Aubrey began to come down, down, fast at first, then slowing as he descended, until he landed with a thump, and found himself in the middle of a boundless world of sand, sky and white, burning sun. In all the silent and blazing lands around him only the desert grasses moved, trembling in the wind.

'Is anybody here?' Aubrey called out.

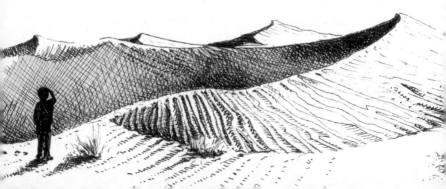

The emptiness of the desert was so perfect that the emptiness itself seemed alive. You would not have been surprised if the air had given a heat-shimmer and emptiness had stepped out of it, like a person coming through a door.

'Oh yes,' said a voice.

There was no one there.

'Where are you?' Aubrey demanded.

'Just here,' said the voice.

'Why can't I see you?'

'I don't want to be seen.'

'Why not?'

There was another listening pause.

'Why NOT?'

'Oh very well,' said the voice, and there was a hissing and a slipping, a slithering sound, and a shape began to resolve in front of him.

Aubrey prepared himself for something huge, something terrible, a thing of vast height and power. He looked around wildly for some sort of weapon, even a stick, but there was nothing. Now the shape was taking form.

At first Aubrey thought it was the shape of a man, but then it hunched over and its shoulders grew huge, like a bear or a giant hyena. Now it changed again, into a twisting thing, something like a tree made of serpents. Now it spindled and legs grew out of it, a writhing scorpion, indistinct. Now it was ragged round the edges and bullish in the centre, now it had eyes, then no eyes, now horns, now none.

'Make up your mind,' Aubrey said, refusing to sound frightened, though his heart was beating fast. 'Stop wriggling about – be something.'

'This is the thing I am,' said the Yoot. 'What do you want with me?'

'I want to fight you,' Aubrey said, 'if you won't go away and leave us alone.'

'You can't beat me and I can't go away,'

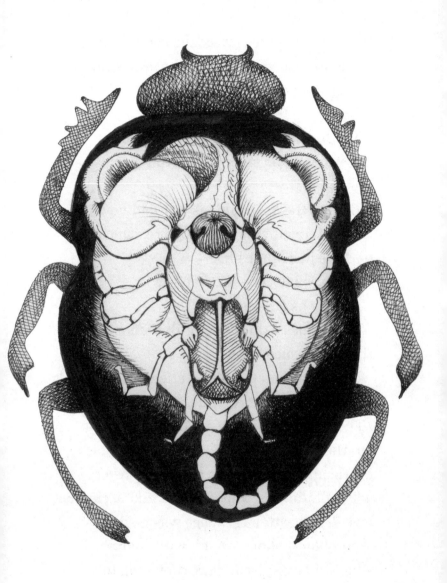

the Yoot answered. It looked something like living barbed wire now, coiling and spiky.

'Why are you picking on my father?'

'Because I like him.'

'You like him? Why do you make him miserable? Do you enjoy making people miserable?'

'Enjoy?' the Yoot said, as if it had never thought about enjoyment before. 'Of course not! It's just what I do.'

'Can't you do something else?'

There was a pause.

'Sometimes I think I can. But when I try...' the Yoot's voice trailed away.

'Don't stop, Yoot!' Aubrey cried. 'Talk to me! What happens when you try?'

There was a pop like a balloon bursting. On the sand dune at his feet a large black beetle appeared. It was about the size of a golf ball. Aubrey bent down to take a closer look. The beetle's carapace was a shiny green-black, shot through with colours which changed from dark ruby reds to gleaming blues.

'Is that you?'

'Yes,' said the beetle.

Aubrey was extremely surprised that such a monster should appear as such a small beast – admittedly quite big for a beetle, but very small indeed compared to what Aubrey had been expecting. He sat down on the sand. The beetle began to run around distractedly until it came upon a lump of dung.

'Camel dung,' it said, almost to itself. The beetle went up onto its front legs, rested its back legs against the dung ball, and by pedalling them it began to roll the dung up the sand dune. Imagine walking backwards on your hands while using your feet to roll a giant beach ball made of muck up a hill. The Beetle-Yoot did this as

though it was perfectly normal.

'What are you doing?' Aubrey asked.

'Exercise,' puffed the beetle.

'Here, let me help,' Aubrey said, reaching for the dung.

'Leave it!' shouted the beetle. 'Don't you understand? Look around – this is the Desert of Misfortune! This is my home!'

The beetle was so worked up it could hardly speak. It heaved and heaved at the ball of dung, pushing it slowly up the dune.

'Tough place to live,' Aubrey said, calmly. 'Why don't you go somewhere else?'

'Tough? It's hell! Nothing here but scorpions and lizards and the occasional camel which drops dung; nothing to do, no one to talk to – and this is where I am from. This is where I am me. Unless I come to your world, and as soon as I do that I am the Terrible Yoot again, the horrendous Terrible Yoot who everyone hates and fears. It's incredibly lonely. And I'm drawn to all sorts of people, good people like Jim, but when they start listening to me you know what happens! EURGH!' shouted the beetle, in a rage.

'So – what are you doing with the dung?' Aubrey asked, gently.

'Pushing it to the top.'

'Then what?'

'Then it will roll back down and I'll go back to the bottom and push it back up to the top again, and so on.'

'I see,' said Aubrey, after a minute.

'It's thrilling,' said the beetle, sulkily. 'It could not be more exciting.'

'And you do it because…?'

'Otherwise I'll go crazy!' cried the beetle. 'Look at my choices! I can sit around here all day, boiling, waiting for the evening when it cools down a bit, and then I can sleep – but if I haven't done anything all day I can't sleep, and then I lie awake having staring competitions with the moon. It never blinks! Or I can go to the world and be a monster.'

The beetle was straining mightily now as it pushed the dung up the dune towards the crest.

'So I roll this – wretched dung – all the way – to the top! There!'

'Well done!' cried Aubrey. Beetle and dung ball rested on the crest, the dung wavering slightly as it balanced on the lip of sand.

'Thanks,' said the beetle, and took its back feet off the dung. The brown matted ball immediately toppled and rolled, faster and faster, with little jumps and bounces, all the way to the bottom, where it came to a stop.

'B minus,' said the beetle. 'When you get a really A-grade ball it's much harder but it rolls further.'

The boy and the beetle looked at the dung, and the beetle sighed and set off back down the dune.

'You know,' said Aubrey, 'you're not horrible at all – to look at –

you're really a very beautiful beetle, with those glowing reds and blues, you're quite magnificent – really specially sort of shiny.'

'Iridescent,' said the beetle. 'When something dark is specially sort of shiny it's called "iridescent". Thank you. This is the only place I can be myself. When I go to the world I'm all those disgusting shapes you saw – whatever people imagine me to be is what I become. You have no idea how ghastly it is to be the worst thing people can imagine.'

'I am sorry, Beetle-Yoot,' Aubrey said. 'I can see it's not your fault. But can't you just stay away from the world?'

The beetle had reached the bottom of the dune now. It manoeuvred itself around the ball, did a handstand, rested its back legs on the ball and gave it a heave.

'I've tried,' it said. 'Believe me, I have tried. But how long could you last here? You try not to, you think of other things – but your mind keeps going back to the world, to all the countries, and the glittering cities, and the great wide sea, and the villages and towns, and all the people with all their lives, and you think, I can't resist it, just a quick look, just a peek to see how they're getting on. I'll just pop over and – as soon as you think it, there you are, and you're looking down on Rushing Wood, for example, and there's Jim, and I like Jim, but the next thing you know you're in his mind. And even if you want to say something kind to him, which I do, it doesn't come out the way you intend. So instead of saying, "You look good today, Jim," you find yourself saying, "That shirt doesn't go with that jacket – can't you find something better?" And it goes on like that, and you're trapped, giving voice to all these horrible thoughts, until you're saying dreadful things to him, and he's miserable! Do you understand? My company is toxic! It's death!'

And with that the beetle stopped pushing and the ball rolled back down and the beetle

threw itself into the sand and howled a
small desperate howl.

'I am only what I AM!' it howled. 'I wish
I was different but I'm NOT. This is ME.
This is MY EXISTENCE! OH HOW I
HATE BEING TRAPPED IN ME!!'

Aubrey couldn't hate a creature in such
misery. Only a short while ago he would
have crushed it under his foot in revenge
for all it had done, but now as the beetle
lay there, pounding its feet against the
sand, Aubrey wanted to help. Gradually the
beetle's tantrum subsided from sobs to sniffs
to a sigh. The boy reached out and stroked
it, running his finger along the beetle's hard
shiny back.

'How did you get your name?' Aubrey
asked.

'I don't know,' the beetle sniffed.

'That might be a clue!' Aubrey said.

'A clue to what?'

'To how we untangle the mystery!'

'What mystery?'

The beetle was looking up at him. It was not a happy beetle, but it was curious now.

'The mystery of your true nature. How can you be such a sensitive beetle, and the Terrible Yoot at the same time? It doesn't make sense, does it?'

'Some things don't,' said the beetle, gloomily.

'Don't be so sure,' Aubrey said. 'Everything makes sense if you can find the right way to look at it. What we need is a new perspective.'

The beetle looked around the Desert of Misfortune. The desiccated bushes waved slightly in the wind.

'Well,' said the beetle, 'I don't know where we're going to find one of those round here.'

The heat and the thinking about the beetle's troubles were making Aubrey's head heavy. He could feel sleep coming for him and he knew that when it reached him he would find himself back in the world.

'Beetle-Yoot,' he said, urgently, 'trust me on this. I know where to go for a new perspective. Keep your spirits up! There is an answer – we will find it. We'll find it, we'll...

...FIND IT!'

...Aubrey cried, sitting upright in bed. It was morning. The garden was sparkling with frost. For all his extraordinary adventures in the night he was not tired at all: he felt as though he had had a deep sleep. 'Right then,' he thought, as he pulled the covers back and swung his legs out of bed. 'A day for new perspectives!'

CHAPTER 13

When the Time is Right

Jim was in a fine mood at breakfast. He had made a pile of bacon, two eggs each, and lots of toast.

'I've made an appointment,' he told Aubrey. 'I'm going to see a special nurse, someone who I can just talk to without worrying that I'm worrying her.'

'Well done, Dad!'

'It's about time,' Jim said. 'You and your mum saved me – really saved me! I feel quite different this morning – and hungry too! Properly hungry for the first time in months!'

Suzanne smiled and took both their hands.

'We're through the worst,' she said. 'From now on things are going to get better. My brave husband and my wonderful son! Better every day, right everybody?'

'Yes!' said Aubrey, but he said it with more conviction than he felt. His father was still shaky, he could see that. Jim was putting on a great show, no doubt about it. He obviously didn't want to worry anyone, and he was definitely better than he had been, but now Aubrey's mind was racing with thoughts of the Beetle-Yoot. How to solve the mystery? And how much time did he have? How long before the Beetle got fed up with rolling dung up sand dunes and came back as the Terrible Yoot?

Jim said he was going to do the housework – he was going to give the whole place a clean, do the laundry and make the house ready for Christmas.

'Then I'm going to plan some lessons for next term,' he said. 'I am going to go back to work, if I feel better, which I'm sure I will.'

'Well,' said Suzanne, 'in that case I'm going to take a proper day off, for once. So I'll see you both later – hurrah! I haven't

had a day off for ages!' She called her friend
Caroline, made plans to go to a gallery later,
packed her swimming things, and away she
went with a wave. Jim started tidying up,
humming to himself. Aubrey put on his coat
and set out for Rushing Wood.

He walked up through the wood, noticing
the holly berries and the frosty moss which
looked like mint ice cream. He climbed up
all the way to the moor and thought back
to the Desert of Misfortune. In daylight,
under a bright sun, the moor looked similar,
icy patches all sparkling and a cold smell of
earth in the air.

'Good morning!' said a musical voice.

A hare hopped out from behind a frozen
tussock. Her fur was a winter patchwork of
whites and browns, which made her almost
invisible. Her eyes were a beautiful dark
gold and the tips of her ears were black.

'Lepus!' Aubrey exclaimed. 'You saved us!'

'Not at all,' Lepus replied, embarrassed,

scratching one long ear with one long hind foot. 'I didn't do anything. How is Jim?'

'He's much better. But now I've got another problem. It's the Beetle-Yoot. If we don't solve his mystery he'll come back and Dad will be in trouble again. I need to talk to someone very wise – could you pass a message to Athene Noctua?'

Lepus twitched her nose.

'Athene gave me a message for you. She said, "When the time is right, go to High Peak. Someone will be there to meet you. And take Jim."'

'Someone – who?'

'Ah, well, someone you should meet, but someone I tend to stay well away from,' Lepus said, and her flanks twitched and the muscles in her long legs tensed, as if she wished she were somewhere else.

'Someone dangerous? Who is it?'

'Ah. Well, she's very big and – rather intimidating. She's visiting from the Far North.'

'How far north?'

'From Furthest North – from the Enchanted Mountains,' said Lepus.

Mr Ferraby lowered his binoculars. He had come up to the moor because a bright winter morning was a very good time for birdwatching. He sometimes saw peregrine falcons going over, looking for grouse. There were no peregrines this morning – just Aubrey, talking with a hare. 'Extraordinary!' he said, and hurried home, unable to keep a word of it to himself a moment longer.

'I've got to tell you!' he cried, bursting into his wife's study. He was so excited he was flushed. 'But you can't tell anyone else! It's just magical!'

'What's that, Athelstan?' Mrs Ferraby asked. She was working on her Master's degree in psychology. She needed peace and quiet.

'Aubrey talks to hares. And squirrels, and that heron – he's best friends with that

heron. I've seen an owl hanging around too
– I bet Aubrey talks to him.'

'You talk to the cat, dear. People talk to
dogs, goldfish, swallows. I've heard Suzanne
talking to the woodpigeons. It obviously
runs in their family.'

'But the animals and birds answer him!
You should have seen him with the hare! A
wild hare, and they were chatting away like
old friends.'

'Have you talked to Aubrey about this?'

'Oh no! No no! No I couldn't. It's his
business. I don't want to embarrass him.
But don't you think it's absolutely amazing?
What a gift! How I'd love to talk to animals!'

'I think you'll be babbling to the bats any
minute now,' Mrs Ferraby said.

Mr Ferraby stared at her. They both
burst into laughter.

'He has an incredible gift, Eunice!
We are living next to the only
boy in Britain who can
talk to animals!

I'm so relieved to have told you. I've been bottling it up – can you imagine the hullabaloo if anyone ever found out? There would be TV people queuing from here to the village. Japanese reporters climbing over the wall, French newscasters pushing offers through the letterbox, satellites buzzing over the house like bees! It would be a perfect nightmare! You won't tell anyone, will you?"

Mrs Ferraby looked her husband right in the eye.

'I won't say a word to anyone about anything, Athelstan,' she said. 'Be-lieve me!'

When the time is right, Aubrey thought to himself, as he made his way home. How will I know when that is?

Maybe I could just ask him one question, or maybe two, Mr Ferraby thought. He doesn't have to answer. I won't pressure him. But I would just love to know something, anything, about what the animals say.

'There's snow on the way,' Jim told Aubrey, as they ate pasta for lunch. 'Huge falls they say on the radio, coming in from the far north. It's going to be a very white Christmas indeed!'

'Coming in from the far north?' Aubrey repeated. 'Is what they said?'

'Yes – it's coming tonight, apparently. I'm

going to go to town and get the stores in. If it's deep the lanes will block. We don't want to carry all the Christmas food up on our backs. Do you want to come and give me a hand?'

Aubrey said he would.

By five o'clock the snow was falling in thick goosefeathers. By seven the street lamp outside seemed to flicker in a whirl of flakes. By nine there was a good inch or two on the ground, and it was still falling. The family had their supper and went to bed.

Aubrey woke up in bed with a start. A noise had brought him up from sleep – was it someone going downstairs? He looked at his clock. Midnight precisely – 00:00, said the numerals, and now one of them changed: 00:01.

'When the time is right,' Aubrey breathed. 'I'll know. It's now!'

He got up and dressed very quietly. He

went downstairs as quietly as a black cat. There was a light shining under the living-room door. He opened it. There, sitting on the sofa, was his father. Jim had his head in his hands. He looked up when Aubrey opened the door.

'Hello, Aubrey Boy!' Jim said, bravely.

'Hello Dad. You OK?'

'Yes!' Jim said. 'Fine!' But he didn't look fine.

Jim smiled. 'I think I must have reversed my clock – can't sleep! Thinking about this and that. Why are you dressed?'

'Come with me, Dad,' Aubrey said. 'We're going for a walk. Let's leave a note for Mum.'

'Are we? OK … why not? A walk in the snow might be lovely.'

As Jim got his boots and coat and hat, and a hat and coat for Aubrey and gloves for both of them, Aubrey wrote Suzanne a note.

Dear Mum we are going for a walk in the snow. Don't worry! We've got all our hats and coats on. We'll be back soonish. There's something I want to show Dad.
Love A xxx

CHAPTER 14

The Visitor from the Furthest North

High Peak is the lighthouse of the moors, a tump of ground which rises to an outcrop of rocks. On a clear day the view is not just spectacular; it is almost supernatural. People have seen remarkable, impossible sights from up there. Walkers have said they looked east and saw right across the country to the North Sea. Lots more have said they looked west and saw the Irish Sea on the other side. Others claim to have seen the Mountains of Mourne in Ireland, and one little girl said she saw all the way to Holland once, in the other direction. 'It was as flat as a slipper and the colour of tulips,' she said. 'And it had windmills.'

To get to High Peak from Woodside Terrace
you cross the stream, climb up the
other side of the valley and take
the road until it runs out. Then
you follow the track until
that runs out and
all you are
left with is a
path. You follow this path
for a while, like Moses crossing
the Red Sea, staying on the
narrow trail
between waves of
moorland, and after a mile
or so there is High Peak,
like a watchtower in the sky.

It was hard work for Jim, and even harder
for Aubrey with his shorter legs, but at least
the snow had stopped falling. There were
clouds, heavy with more goosefeathers,
driving southwards overhead. Here and
there were ragged gaps where starlight
showed, and the luminous snow gathered

every photon of light, collected it and bounced it back at the clouds, so that Jim and Aubrey walked over a glowing white moor, under clouds like a swollen sea. Star patches rode in this sea above them like islands. The snow crunched softly under their feet.

'Where are you taking me, Aubrey Boy?'

'Guess!'

'I think I know...'

'You probably do.'

'Feel like a view, eh Aubrey? I doubt we'll see Holland tonight.'

'There's someone we've got to meet.'

'Really?' cried Jim, alarmed. 'In the middle of the night? Who?'

'A Visitor from Furthest North,' Aubrey said. 'I've never met her before.'

'Not someone you met on the internet?' Jim demanded, 'Not some crazy kook?'

Aubrey decided his father needed to know one or two things.

'Dad, you know the heron? His name's

Ardea. He's a friend of mine, right?'

Jim laughed. 'That makes sense!' he exclaimed. 'Well, not sense exactly but...'

'And you know the raven and the squirrels, and Marcel the fly? They're sort of my friends too.'

Jim nodded. He might have been having a bad time recently but he was still a man who understood stories very well, and knew there were more stories in even the smallest wood than could ever be written or imagined.

'I'd like to meet them,' Jim said. 'Except that raven! I've had plenty of him! But I guess they don't talk to everyone?'

Aubrey was extremely relieved. 'This is that kind of friend. We'll recognise her when we see her, according to Athene.'

'Got you,' said Jim. 'Who is Athene? Some sort of owl?'

'Some sort is right,' Aubrey grinned.

The last scramble up the side of High Peak made them both pant. They were not far from the top when Aubrey stopped.

'Dad! Look! She's there!'

Jim peered ahead. He could see the outcrop of stones that marked the highest point but there was nothing ... wait! There *was* something there. Perching on the stones themselves was a shape, a huge, mantled shape like an eagle, but white, white as the moor.

'It's a...' Jim gasped.

'She's a...' Aubrey panted.

'She's a Snowy Owl!' Jim whispered. 'I – they hardly ever – it's incredible! They hardly ever come to this country – *what a blessing!* We'd better not get too close or we'll scare her away.'

'We won't,' Aubrey said. 'Come on, we'll talk to her.'

'You really think…?'

'Yes, yes!'

'Yes,' said a deep gentle voice. 'Come up.'

'That was *her*?' Jim squeaked.

Jim and Aubrey climbed together, holding hands, until they arrived at the top of High Peak and stood before the great Snowy Owl. Close up they could see she had riffles of black feathers among the white, and her eyes were like huge amber lanterns. Her beak was shiny black and her feet were tufted with thick white feathers, as if she were wearing plump slippers. Shiny black talons, sharp as scimitars, curved out of her toes.

The Snowy Owl squeezed her yellow eyes

at them in an owl smile. 'My name is Scandiacus,' she said, 'but my friends call me Bubo. Now, why have I come to see you?'

Aubrey cleared his throat. 'Ahem, um, hello – Bubo! I think you have come to help us with the Terrible Yoot – have you?'

'Only you can help yourselves with him,' said the owl. 'But I can help you help yourselves. Why is he troubling you?'

'He says he's lonely, and he likes Dad!'

'What is this Yoot?' Jim asked. Although he could hear Bubo and Aubrey talking telepathically he asked the question aloud. Aubrey answered him the same way.

'The Terrible Yoot is the voice in your head that has been making you so sad,' Aubrey told him. 'He's the source of all your troubles, but he's only a small dung beetle in the other world, and he's lonely there, but when he comes here he becomes this monster and when he tries to be kind to you it comes out all wrong and tortures you.'

'A dung beetle?'

Jim looked dazed.

'What do you want to know about him?' Bubo asked.

'Why is he called the Yoot?'

'Ah! That is the question! How do you spell his name?'

'Why oh oh tee,' Aubrey said.

Bubo smiled again. 'Do you know the difference between an acronym and a proper noun?' she asked.

'Uum … an acronym is … some sort of symptom?' Aubrey guessed. 'Like spots?'

'No!' Jim cried, 'An acronym is made of the first letters of a series of words, like radar comes from the first letters of RAdio Detection And Ranging. Or FAQ – Frequently Asked Question. A proper noun is a name for a thing or person, like Aubrey.'

'Dad's an English teacher,' Aubrey explained.

Bubo shuffled her feathers. 'Yoot is not a proper noun, it's an acronym.'

'We need to know what it stands for then!'

Aubrey exclaimed.

'What might it stand for?' Bubo returned.

'Yowl oh oh terrible? You orange or terror? You oink oink tomorrow?'

'Do you know what a homophone is?' asked the owl, rising up slightly. She looked enormous. It was like being tested by a huge headmistress with a massive beak and claws, Aubrey thought. Don't be scared, he told himself, you can deal with owls.

'Go on Aubrey,' Jim said. 'Try!'

'Is it – like a xylophone?'

'Nearly!' Jim said. *'Xylo* means wood in Greek, *phone* is sound. Xylophone is 'woodsound'. *Homo* means "same" in Greek, so homophone is "same sound". A word that sounds the same as another word.'

'Correct!' said Bubo, with a low purring sound. She reminded Aubrey of other great hunters he had seen on television. She was like a lion or something. But owlish...

'Yes,' Jim said. 'Homophones are words with the same sound but different meanings and often a different spelling.'

Aubrey saw it now. 'So his name sounds like Yoot but it's not spelt Y-O-O-T ... how is it spelt?'

'Y-U-T-E?' Jim guessed.

'Shorter!' hooted the owl.

'U-T-E!'

cried Aubrey.

'Indeed!' said Bubo. 'So what does it stand for?'

'Utterly Terrible Evil?' Aubrey tried.

'But's he's not evil, is he?' Bubo prompted, gently.

Aubrey thought. 'I was sure he was until I met him. He does evil things but not in his world, and he doesn't mean to, I believe that – so, he's – not exactly evil, no.'

'You have one word right, but you need to swap the adjectival form for the noun.'

'Dad? Help!'

'Well,' Jim said, 'utterly is an adverb, you know because it ends in -ly. Evil is a noun *and* an adjective and anyway you say this thing isn't evil, though it feels pretty evil to me. But if it's not that then it must be terrible. If terrible is the adjective, what is the noun?'

'Nouns and adjectives!' Aubrey cried. 'Why can't they all go and boil their heads!'

Bubo narrowed her eyes at the

boy. Jim shook his head. 'Terror,' he said, patiently. 'The noun is terror.'

'Ugly terror enemy!' Aubrey guessed, excited now.

Bubo's eyes narrowed. 'Was he really ugly, when you met him in the desert?'

Aubrey paused. 'No – not at all. He was just trapped in his existence.'

'Existence!' repeated the owl. 'Two words right.'

'U-something Terror Existence – what is U?'

'U is everything,' said Bubo.

'Universal,' Jim said, instantly. 'It's the only U that means everything.'

'Correct,' said the owl. 'And there's an 'of' in there too.'

'Universal Terror of Existence,' Aubrey said, slowly. 'He's the Universal Terror of Existence? What is that?'

'What does it sound like? Think.'

Bubo ruffled her feathers and spun her head around, looking far into the night. Aubrey turned away. The snow was not falling now. There was no wind. The moor sparkled all the way to the clouds. What was the Universal Terror of Existence? Jim put his arms over Aubrey's shoulders, so that Aubrey stood with his back to his father, keeping warm.

'It's something everyone has,' Aubrey said, 'if it's universal.'

'That makes sense to me,' Jim said. 'I've been feeling terrified in my existence, but I didn't think of being terrified *of* it.'

'If you didn't exist you wouldn't be terrified,' Aubrey thought aloud.

'And I didn't want to exist,' Jim agreed. 'I thought I was too terrified to live. In fact the real terror came when I realised I wanted to live and I thought it was too late.'

'So – existence means terror?' Aubrey frowned. 'Isn't that a bit bleak?'

'Let me show you a thing or two about bleak,' said Bubo. 'Look that way, what do you see?'

Aubrey and Jim followed the direction of

the owl's gaze. The moors fell away to the south, low horizontals of snow running to the sky.

'Just the moors and the cloud,' Aubrey said. 'Nothing much.'

'Bleak?' Bubo enquired.

'Pretty bleak!' Aubrey laughed.

'Now watch,' said the owl.

The Snowy Owl drew herself up in a stretch, like someone straightening her back, and spun her head, first to the left, then to the right, so that her blazing gaze swept all the moors around. Now she looked south and hunched forward, as if she were about to take off, and dug her mighty talons into the crevices of her perch. Her wings unfurled and she began to beat them; to Aubrey it was as though a great bluster of icy wind had erupted around him, but then, instead of freezing him, it seemed to stream away towards the skyline. As he watched, the miracle began.

CHAPTER 15
The Miracle

The owl's wingbeats sent a scoop of air towards the distant clouds in an invisible stream. When it reached the clouds, this stream seemed to furl them up, like a breeze lifting a great curtain. The clouds' edges tore and twisted, rising, splitting, dissolving, as if all the snow they contained had melted at once, leaving only a wide clear in the sky. In this clear air was a pure twinkling sky so full of stars they seemed like nets of light. Further and further the wide clear spread, until the whole horizon was serene and perfect.

'Like the first night on earth!' Aubrey whispered.

It was as though they stood in a gigantic cathedral with the whole galaxy for a roof, where the planets were gold and crimson

pearls. All around them starlight shimmered
on the snow like notes of music they could
not quite hear.

'How far can you see?' asked Bubo
Scandiacus, very softly.

'There's Woodside Terrace, and there's the
village,' Aubrey said. 'And there's the town,
and the railway line, and the city – I can
see the whole city! It looks tiny, like crushed
jewels, all those lights – and beyond – look at
that huge mountain! What's that?'

'It can't be Snowdon,' Jim said, not quite
believing it. 'But it can only be Snowdon!'

And there it was, the mountain's towering
crest shining like an iceberg, and all around
it were the mountains of Wales,
rising like dolphins into the
glittering night.

'And that's the coast! Isn't it, Dad? It must be, look, you can see the line of lights along the shore, and those flashes, red and green...'

'They're buoys!' Jim exclaimed, 'Navigation lights for the ships coming in from the west...'

'I can see ships,' Aubrey cried, 'on *both* sides, look over there! Those are the lights of the east coast, aren't they? Isn't that a lighthouse?'

'Yes, and beyond it that's a lighthouse on the *other* side, the Dutch coast, the other side of the North Sea,' Jim said, and his voice was shaky now, because not only could they both see, quite clearly, the coasts of France

and Holland to the east, they could also see the lights of Ireland to the west, and there were the Mountains of Mourne, and as Aubrey stared he saw the mighty Atlantic on the further side, furrowed with the infinite ripples of its waves, where the moon like a sea creature rose out of the ocean and laid a silvering path upon it, all the way to America.

Aubrey hardly dared to keep staring, because everywhere he turned his gaze, the distances fell away. Now he looked east, and there were the dark fields of France, and if he focused he could see tiny villages, churches and canals, and there was a city with a white-domed cathedral on a hill, and a million rooftops, and a river which bent around a tower which flashed like a firework.

'The Eiffel Tower!' he exclaimed. 'It must be Paris!

And now he looked west, and tracking across the ocean he followed the wakes of ships, and over the curve of the world he saw glowing and pulsing miniature towers which must be huge, huge skyscrapers, and a city of bridges and reefs of light.

'Dad,' Aubrey said, seriously, 'I can see New York!'

And they both started to laugh, because it was impossible, but they could both see the towers and the lights and the bridges, as clearly as you can see the words on this page.

'What can you see?' asked Bubo Scandiacus.

'I can see – everything!' Aubrey said. 'I mean I can see about seven countries, and two seas, and the whole ocean, and all the way to America. It's some sort of spell.'

'Only a very simple spell,' the owl replied. 'What you are seeing is always there. It's only slightly unusual to see it all at once.'

'You can never see all this at once!'

'You can if you fly high enough. And now you have seen it you will never forget it, will you?'

'No way! I'll always remember it. I don't

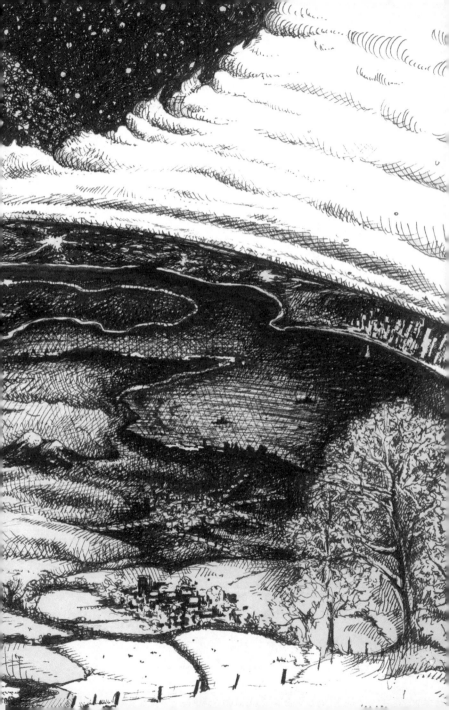

want to stop looking – could I see Africa?'

'Yes, if you look south east, do you see those peaks, like a tiny white saw on its back?'

'Yes!'

'Those are the Pyrenees – that's Spain beyond. Do you see the high plains, and the mountains? And the sea beyond them?'

'Yes! I can see two mountains, one further away...'

'That is Jebel Musa. That's in Africa.'

'Dad, I can see Africa!'

'So can I,' Jim said, 'And no one will ever believe us!'

'Mum will. But I can't believe it – I can't believe how beautiful it all is,' Aubrey said, and he wanted to cry, for the wonder of the world was almost overwhelming.

'And to think it's always there, but we can't see it!'

'But you do see it,' said the owl. 'You see it in miniature every time you go outside and look at what the world *is*. This is what exists – this is EXISTENCE! This is, you are, I am, we are, existence! And this is the world as it is.'

'As you never see it,' Aubrey said.

'Hoot! If you fly as high as a space rocket you can see all this. If you fly as high as a satellite you can see whole countries in a glance. If you only fly as high as an aeroplane you will see that it is always a sunny day above the clouds. Or a clear night.'

'What does this have to do with the Yoot?' Aubrey asked, forgetting the new spelling, because he was concentrating on seeing how far into Africa he could see, which turned out to be very far – his gaze was travelling across the Sahara desert now, and he could see a dark jungle on the far side where he thought there must be elephants.

'With the Universal Terror of Existence, I mean. How does it help us with that?'

Bubo Scandiacus the Snowy Owl smiled an owl smile that Aubrey felt but did not see, because now his gaze was crossing the great plains of Africa, where he could make out giraffes sleeping among the trees.

'What are the two sides of the Yoot?' she asked.

'Huge monster and tiny beetle,' Aubrey said, without thinking.

'And what are the two sides of existence?'

'Oh it's ... huge ... beautiful ... infinite ... *infinite* wonder,' Aubrey said, dreamily.

He was looking diagonally across the whole of Africa to the Indian Ocean, where he could see the spouts of whales, and their great flipping tails.

'Yes – and the other side?'

'Terror and fear,' said Jim, in a low voice.

'True,' said the owl. 'So how do you live with both of them, then?'

'Easy!' Aubrey exclaimed. 'If I ever meet the monster, I will remember the beetle. And I will talk to the beetle in the monster.'

'Yes!' Jim cried, in his excited teacher way, 'And if I meet terror and fear I will know they are only the other side of infinite wonder, and I will try to look past the fear to the wonder!'

'Then,' said the great owl, 'you have seen the miracle and you have learned the secret. When you wake up you will remember everything. I wish you peace ... and Merry Christmas!'

Jim and Aubrey do not know how long they stood there, staring across the whole world. When they got home it was Christmas morning. First they had to tell Suzanne all about their adventure. Aubrey knew she would believe them, and she did.

Later on there was a knock on the door which turned out to be a very pleasant man from France named Serge who worked for a television station. He had heard a rumour that there was a boy in Woodside Terrace who could talk to animals.

Aubrey explained that he did not talk to animals, he communicated with them in his mind. Serge might have been a bit disappointed but he did not show it, which was remarkable considering how far he had come.

'I am based in London,' he said. 'But in my job if it is a huge story like this one – like this one could 'ave been – you 'ave to go whatever day it is. I have brought my wife, Francine, and my daughter, Esmeralda.'

'You must all come in and have lunch with us!' Suzanne said.

So Serge and Francine and Esmeralda did. Esmeralda was Aubrey's age exactly. She spoke perfect English with a French accent and sometimes added French words to her sentences. They were both rather shy but they smiled at each other as they all sat down to the feast Suzanne and Jim had made.

After lunch Mr and Mrs Ferraby came round with presents. Mr Ferraby and Serge seemed to know each other somehow, and Mrs Ferraby spoke excellent French, so she was soon chatting away with Francine, and Suzanne and Jim served everyone mulled wine. Then they stood talking to their guests, Jim's arm around Suzanne's shoulder, and they looked very happy. 'Would you like to see the garden?' Aubrey asked Esmeralda. 'It's quite good in the snow.'

'Ah *oui* – yes please!' Esmeralda said.

They slipped out through the back door and walked through the garden, noting the bright red berries of the hawthorn, and the pink Christmas roses, and the mistletoe in the plum tree. They paused at the pond, which was frozen icy green.

'Is it true you can talk to animals, O-bree?' Esmeralda asked.

She pronounced his name O-bree. He liked the way she said it.

'In a way,' Aubrey said. 'It's hard to explain. I hear their voices in my mind and I answer with my thoughts.'

He thought Esmeralda would think that was silly but instead she nodded.

'What do they say?' she asked.

'It depends,' Aubrey said, feeling foolish. 'On the animal and the subject.'

Esmeralda laughed and pointed at something on top of the post at the edge of the wood. 'So what does that insect say?'

Aubrey looked closer. On top of the fence post was a large green-black beetle, shining – iridescent.

'It's the Yoot! And he's come as a beetle, not a monster at all! How amazing – hello Yoot!' he said. 'Look at you – how wonderful!'

Esmeralda watched closely. The beetle waved his antennae at Aubrey, exactly as if he was replying.

'What is he saying, O-bree?'

'He says he is glad he knows now what his name means, and that there are two sides to him. He can come here now as himself, not as the monster. It's complicated. He says he would like to be friends,' Aubrey explained, 'if we don't mind. And he thinks you're very pretty and very clever.'

Aubrey blushed as he said it, and Esmeralda laughed.

'He is a most polite beetle,' she said. 'Of course we can be friends. What's he saying now?'

'Christmas cake,' Aubrey said. 'He says if we have any spare, he would love to try it. He's never had it before. And – oh! Oh. Never mind.'

'*Quoi?* What was that?' Esmeralda asked, keenly, and she laughed at Aubrey with her eyes, it seemed to him.

'Nothing,' Aubrey said. 'Nothing much. Shall we get some cake?'

'Yes,' said Esmeralda. 'But wait ... I like this garden.'

'Me too!' Aubrey said, feeling full of joy. 'Let's make a snowman! I mean, we could, if you like?'

As he said it he thought Esmeralda might feel it was a babyish idea but her face lit up immediately.

'We can make a snow beetle,' she said. 'We can make him *enorme.*'

And so Aubrey and Esmeralda began to make the biggest snow beetle the world had ever seen, and the iridescent insect watched them from the top of his post, and the world turned, and later on everyone had Christmas cake – even the Terrible Yoot, for the first time in his existence, which was not so terrible now. Esmeralda and Aubrey got on very well. Esmeralda turned out to be just as rambunctious as Aubrey. (She had a laugh like a wild goblin.) Indeed, as she whispered to him, there was only one thing

in the whole world that made her scared –
araignees! Which is a French word, and she
told Aubrey what it means. Aubrey said he
would try to help her with the *araignees,*
though he was a bit scared of them too. But
that is another adventure, for another time.

FOOTNOTE: Aubrey will return in

AUBREY AND THE
TERRIBLE PIDERS!

ACKNOWLEDGEMENTS

CREATORS: Jane Matthews, genius, Robin Tetlow-Shooter, Penny Thomas and Claire Brisley made it come true. Rebecca Shooter has had my back through thick and thin. I will love you always. Thank you, darling. Jennifer Shooter: if not for you we would be so busy looking after Aubrey we would have run out of work and money a long time ago. Thank you. Aubrey Shooter Clare: I borrowed your name and six-week-old character. This book is for you.

Sally, John and Alexander Clare; Roy, Sarah, Cynthia and Sheila Clare; Emily Simonis; Ursula, Ben & Hugh Williams, Sophie and Richard, William and Twins, Martina and Niamh Williams, Sian, Ioan and Ffyon Williams; Gerald, Emma and Chris and Jamie Shooter – what a family! Geoffrey Williams and Janey Clare we miss and love.

MAKERS: Lexie Hamblin of Rogers Coleridge & White: the first person after Penny to believe in it. Thank you so much, Lexie! Zoe Waldie, greatest agent, just keeps guiding me. Thank you Zo! If anyone reads this book it will be due to Megan Farr, Michael Morpurgo and Frank Cottrell Boyce. Thank you.

FRIENDS: Roger Couhig, Merlin Hughes, Anna Rose Hughes, Elizabeth Mann, James Mann, Mike White, Sadie Campbell, Chris Kenyon, Suzanne Fogg, incredible Diarmaid Gallacher, Candace and Taylor Cade, Mary Generelli, Flavio Dossi, Alison 'Tig' Finch, Sally Spurring, Mo Bakaya, Rob Ketteridge, Sarah Dunant and the Great

Ant, Hannah Duguid, Jeremy Grange, Dominic Williams, Menna Elfyn, Anthony Trance Jones, Julian May, Seamus May, Sarah Hemming, Adele Gardner, Tom Morris, Sandeep Parmar, Elizabeth Passey, Lawrence Pollard, Peter Florence, Becky Shaw, Carole Williams, Henry Howard, Megan Lloyd, Kevin Jackson, Deryn Rees Jones, Barnaby Rogerson, Rose Baring, Ben Hardiman, EJ Major and God's Own Rev Richard Coles, whether you knew it or not, you kept me going. Thank you.

WRITERS & TEACHERS: Rupert Crisswell, John Venning, Ken Corn, Peter Browne, Niall Griffiths, Debs Jones, Julia Bell, Jay Griffiths, Jim Perrin, Sian Walker, Jan Morris, Anne Garwood, Robert Macfarlane, Anna Gavalda and Lady Laura Barton: the things you send and say have meant it all. It is an honour to be in the same trades as you, at the same time. Gods love you and thank you, with all my heart.

SECRET SPIRITS: Janey Clare and Thomas Schmidt, who met once in this world (special friends, surely, in the next) we pray you rest in joy and peace. Amen.

www.fireflypress.co.uk